THE CROSSED-OUT NOTEBOOK

A Novel

NICOLÁS GIACOBONE

Translated by Megan McDowell

SCRIBNER

New York   London   Toronto   Sydney   New Delhi

Scribner
An Imprint of Simon & Schuster, Inc.
1230 Avenue of the Americas
New York, NY 10020

Originally published in 2018 in Spain by Penguin Random House Grupo Editorial,
S. A. U., as *El cuaderno tachado*

First Scribner hardcover edition September 2019

For information about special discounts for bulk purchases,
please contact Simon & Schuster Special Sales at 1-866-506-1949
or business@simonandschuster.com.

The Simon & Schuster Speakers Bureau can bring authors to your live event.
For more information or to book an event, contact the Simon & Schuster Speakers
Bureau at 1-866-248-3049 or visit our website at www.simonspeakers.com.

Interior design by Kyle Kabel

Manufactured in the United States of America

1   3   5   7   9   10   8   6   4   2

Library of Congress Cataloging-in-Publication Data has been applied for.

ISBN 978-1-5011-9874-8
ISBN 978-1-5011-9876-2 (ebook)

THE CROSSED-OUT NOTEBOOK

THE CROSSED-OUT NOTEBOOK

It all started with a screenplay.

A screenplay I should never have written.

Amadeus is a great screenplay.

I read it more than a dozen times, studied it, chewed it up and swallowed it, then I stuck my fingers down my throat.

Amadeus was a good play, then it became a great screenplay.

The screenplay far surpasses the play.

Peter Shaffer surpassed himself by turning his own good play into his own (or sort of his own) great screenplay.

While he was writing the play, Peter Shaffer could never have imagined that F. Murray Abraham would later do what he did before the cameras that filmed his screenplay; he was completely unaware that his play was going to end up a movie, and that the movie was going to win everything, and that F. Murray Abraham was going to put body and soul into the greatest exegesis ever seen of the struggle between an artist and his irrevocable mediocrity.

What name does the "F" in F. Murray Abraham hide?

Ferdinand?

Filomeno?

Federico?

Santiago Salvatierra says the "F" doesn't mean anything, that F. Murray Abraham's real name is Murray Abraham, and that Murray added the "F" because he thought it would sound better.

Santiago told me that F. Murray Abraham is a despicable person.

I asked him how he knew that, and he looked at me the way he looks at me when I ask him a question he doesn't want me to ask, and he left the basement and shut the door.

F. Murray Abraham is a despicable genius, he'd said.

But aren't we all despicable in some way or other?

That's not the problem, no; the problem is that the majority of us are not geniuses.

The *vast* majority.

Peter Shaffer is a genius.

Is?

Was?

Peter Shaffer wrote his play, and then his screenplay, on a typewriter in a comfortable office with large windows and lamps of all sizes for the sunless hours.

I live in a basement.

Five years, I've lived in this basement.

I have a lamp that illuminates little to nothing.

I write in this notebook from six in the morning to seven in the morning.

Then I spend a few minutes crossing out what I've written, just before Santiago comes down with his chair, a cup of coffee, a dish of fruit, and printed-out scenes with his scribbled notes: margins full of comments that are usually deplorable.

This thing you are reading now (if there is a you) is nothing but crossed-out words, a text scrawled hurriedly in a Rivadavia school notebook that I brought with me from Buenos Aires.

Text in blue ink, camouflaged by neat lines of black ink that cross it out.

I am forty-five years old.

I've been writing for twenty years.

Though during those first few years I didn't write, I *tried* to write.

I tried for eight, nine hours a day.

When I finished high school, I enrolled at the Buenos Aires School of Music.

I wanted to be a session musician.

Instrument of choice: guitar.

But you don't get to be a session musician when you start at nineteen.

I didn't even come close.

I fled the conservatory before I finished my second year, sick and tired of seeing and hearing those kids who were still in elementary school play their instruments as if they were natural extensions of their arms and legs and mouths.

In my hands, the guitar was an imposture.

I don't know if "imposture" is the right word.

It sounds good.

Every morning, after breakfast—Dolca instant coffee with milk and three Lincoln biscuits that I dipped in the coffee and milk until they fell apart—I'd lock myself into my room (my tiny room that fit only a short, narrow bed, the Marshall amp I'd bought in thirty-six installments, the stand with sheet music and exercises in auditory perception and musical literacy, the four-tiered Technics stereo I bought in twenty-four installments, and some books and albums scattered over the floor), I'd pick up the Mexican Fender Stratocaster that I'd bought in twelve installments, and my hands would need at least half an hour to figure out what that long object I was forcing them to manhandle was.

When I accepted my failure as a music student and my lack of a future as a session musician, my parents, as any parents anywhere in the world would do, asked me what I planned to do with my life:

What are your plans? We want to help you, but we need to know what you plan to do, what you *want* to do. We need to be sure that you know what it is you want to do.

I told them that, unfortunately, I didn't have the slightest idea.

They didn't like it when I told them that.

For twenty minutes, in silence, they concentrated on their roast beef with pureed squash; they didn't look at me; they didn't look at each other; their eyes flitted from nothing to their plates and back to nothing.

My old man worked for a millionaire who owned twenty-five percent of the world's duty-free shops.

His job was to evaluate the employees.

He traveled once a month, mainly to cities in Latin America and Europe, where he would settle into a hotel near the airport and he'd spend two days going to the various duty-free shops, jotting down details both spatial and human in a little notebook with a cream-colored cover.

He was obsessive about order and cleanliness, a fanatical believer in his own way of seeing things.

I went with him only once, to Rio de Janeiro.

He went up to one of the employees of the largest duty-free shop in the Tom Jobim International Airport, and, in perfect Portuguese, asked him why the bottles of Johnnie Walker Red were on the shelf above the bottles of Johnnie Walker Black, when clearly Johnnie Walker Red was of inferior quality to Johnnie Walker Black; and not only that, but why were the bottles of Johnnie Walker Red in their boxes while the Johnnie Walker Black bottles were not, when there was nothing impressive about the Johnnie Walker Red boxes, they didn't catch your attention in the slightest, while the Johnnie Walker Black boxes immediately seduced you with their golden contours and golden letters, and the finish on their boxes was so much glossier, so much more striking, than the Johnnie Walker Red's?

The employee stood for a long while without saying a word, staring at my father as if he were a serial killer calmly explaining how he planned to murder the employee, along with his family, and how he planned to dispose of the bodies.

Years later, on one of those flights, my old man got up to pee in the middle of the night, went into the plane's little bathroom, closed the door, and, while he was peeing, rested his forehead against the curved wall. But before he finished squeezing out the last drops, the plane jolted furiously in a sudden bout of turbulence; my old man's head was still resting against the curved wall, his thoughts who knows where, and his neck snapped.

We want to help you, son, my parents said.

It was strange for them to call me "son."

My parents had called me "son" very rarely.

They called me "son" one night when I was sixteen years old, at the Italian Hospital, after I got into a car wreck on Libertador with my only friend, Lisandro.

We had downed a bottle of Smirnoff vodka mixed with Sprite and Minerva lemon juice.

The right front wheel grazed the guardrail, and the car spun approximately two hundred forty degrees, and another car that was coming too fast rammed into our trunk; we shot ahead, squeezed and speeding at the same time, and something exploded in one of our cars, but miraculously no one was gravely injured.

You nearly scared us to death, son.

My old lady had wanted to be an actress, and for over a decade she'd struggled to become an actress, until she got sick of the struggle and she and two friends started dressing up as Disney characters at children's birthday parties.

It was successful.

Very successful.

So much so that five years ago, when I got onto the plane that carried me to San Martín de los Andes and ultimately into Santiago Salvatierra's basement, my old lady, who was almost seventy years old, was still making her living from the children's birthday party act, not as a performer but as the coordinator of a group of young actors and actresses who, like her, had struggled to make it in theater, film, and television, and had almost always been rudely rejected by the theater, film, and television.

When my old man passed away, my old lady and I moved to a smaller apartment, where we shared a king-sized bed that barely left enough room for us to open the closet doors.

After I fled the Buenos Aires School of Music, I spent several years with no idea what to do with myself.

I lived with my mother, and I had breakfast and dinner with my mother, and during the day I went to a café to read.

I read anything and everything.

I always carried around a used book, and when I finished it, I would trade it in for another used book.

In the evenings, I'd meet up with my friend Lisandro to eat or drink something.

A cup of coffee.

Sometimes a Fernet and Coke.

Swiss chocolate ice cream with strawberry sorbet.

If I met a girl in one of those cafés or bars or ice cream shops, I'd pray that she had her own place, somewhere we could be alone, that if she lived with her family she would at least have a room where she and I could lock ourselves away.

I didn't meet many girls, and the few I did meet dumped me as soon as they found out I shared a bed with my old lady.

It was hopeless.

They didn't even care when I showed them it was a king-sized bed, so big that my old lady and I never even touched during the night.

I don't have a real bed here in the basement.

It took Santiago several days just to bring down a mattress.

He waited until I'd handed over the finished first act.

He waited until he'd made sure the first act worked, that *I* worked.

Now I spend my nights on a mattress that Santiago tells me used to belong to his son, Hilario.

A fickle kid (says Santiago) who can't focus on something, anything, for more than five minutes. Not five fucking minutes. A kid who draws like the gods, has an innate talent for drawing, but is not the slightest bit interested in drawing. Not the slightest bit interested in anything.

I told Santiago that when I was Hilario's age, I wasn't interested in anything, either. Not a thing. And that my old lady had suffered a lot because of that.

But at least you read, he told me. You could finish a book, or learn a song on the guitar. This brat's no good even for boiling an egg. He gets bored halfway through. And the egg is just left there, overcooking, until it breaks and the white gets all foamy.

You have to give him time.

Time? He's about to turn twenty-five years old.

Twenty-five is the new fifteen.

NICOLÁS GIACOBONE

Says who?

I don't know.

Sounds like bullshit to me.

Santiago has spent time living in Spain, Mexico, Venezuela, Ecuador, Cuba, a few months in Bolivia, Peru, Chile, Paraguay, Uruguay, three weeks in Jamaica, two in Panama, and a few days in Colombia.

He built his reputation as the greatest Latin American film director of all time by draining the coffers of the cinematic institutes of Spanish-speaking countries, winning folks over with his warm and expansive personality, his endless smooth talk.

Santiago Salvatierra is among the greatest directors of all time—the real and true greats.

His camerawork and his commitment with the actors—the demands he places on them—are unparalleled.

He is a blend of colossal energy and good taste—*excellent* taste.

A glut of talent that he applies to the visual field.

His shots spill from the screen, they splash you, they mess up your hair, they embrace you, they whisper into your ear.

Santiago was born to direct film.

He was built for the sole purpose of standing behind a camera.

From the cradle.

No formal education required.

An ambitious autodidact.

A flesh-and-blood balloon loaded with eternal images.

Santiago's problem is that he can't write.

His genius, the one that bursts from the screen, vanishes at the sight of a blank page.

Santiago is two artists at once: the director who breakfasts with Fellini and Kurosawa, and the screenwriter who timidly opens the door to the writing workshop and sits at a table with six bored housewives.

8

No, Santiago's problem isn't that he can't write.

A lot of directors can't write.

Santiago's problem is that *he thinks* he can write.

He fancies himself a screenwriter.

He fancies himself an auteur, in the fullest sense of the word.

Many directors believe themselves to be auteurs in the fullest sense of the word, as if it weren't enough to just be a director, as if directing a film they didn't write meant directing someone else's film, or a film that wasn't all theirs, as if a movie written by one person and directed by another was authorless, an orphan; or worse, as if it had several adoptive parents—a child with too many mothers.

Most directors can't write.

I'd bet the little I have left—which is the hope that my mother is still alive—that I'm right about that.

Ninety-nine percent of directors can't write.

No one will care that I say this.

Who's going to take the trouble to read what I've written and crossed out in this notebook?

Who really wants to decipher crossed-out text?

Ninety-nine point four percent of directors can't write.

So what?

Don't worry, directors.

There are thousands of screenwriters scattered around, living in ditches like Beckett characters, just waiting for the chance to help you out.

The movie will still be yours, all yours, plus a tiny bit ours.

Put your name nice and big on the poster.

Just don't try to do what we can do and you can't; don't be so smug as to believe that writing a screenplay is something anyone can do.

Ninety-nine point two percent of directors think it's possible to write like Peter Shaffer, that it's just a matter of sitting down and doing it, a matter of reading a couple of books about the basic rules of screenwriting, and that's that.

* * *

Santiago just left with his chair.

He came down with the cup of coffee, the little dish of fruit, and the printouts of the scenes with his notes.

Of his more than forty notes, there were only three worthwhile.

Like he does every morning, Santiago came down into the basement, turned on the light, walked over to the mattress, and held the cup of hot coffee under my nose.

Like I do every morning, I pretended to be asleep.

Then we sat down (him in his chair and me on the mattress) to discuss his notes.

Over time, over the course of the two screenplays I've written in the basement, I've learned that it's best not to oppose Santiago, not to reject his suggestions outright even if they are completely wrong—as suggestions tend to be when people who don't know how to write critique a written text.

Over time I've learned that you can write a good version of just about anything, that the best approach is to take the note (not literally), mull it over, and rummage around in it until I find what the note got right (right for me, not for Santiago), what the note contains that doesn't upset what has been written, but rather enriches it.

An exhausting process, I'll admit.

But all collaboration is exhausting.

It *has* to be.

At least, all collaboration between two artists who value each other.

Two artists who aren't Siamese twins separated at birth.

This is the third screenplay I've written for Santiago.

The two previous ones, as is well known (though it's not well known that I was the one who wrote them), wrenched Latin American cinema from its slumber and set movie theaters on fire.

Not only were Santiago Salvatierra's last two films extraordinary successes at the box office, they also won the lion's share of all awards in existence, from the Palme d'Or at Cannes, to the Goyas, the BAFTAs, the Golden Globes, and culminating, for both movies, with the Best Foreign Language Film at the Oscars.

It was the third time in history that a director won two Oscars in a row for Best Foreign Film; the other two: Ingmar Bergman and Federico Fellini.

But this third screenplay is the hardest.

This third screenplay is the one that, in Santiago's words: will win everything.

Every. Thing.

And when Santiago says "ev-er-y-thing," he is specifically referring to Hollywood.

This third screenplay (that is, the movie that will come from this screenplay) is the one that will set movie theaters ablaze in the United States, that will break all box office records, even in countries like Japan and China, and that will sweep the Golden Globes and the Oscars in the general categories, and won't be reduced to the category of Foreign Language Film.

According to Santiago, this film is going to be so big that the award won't even matter.

In addition to best film and best director, and best actor and actress, and best supporting actor and actress, and best cinematography, and best soundtrack, Santiago's last two films, the ones I wrote for him, won several awards for best screenplay.

Santiago has won several awards as a screenwriter.

His madness, or his ego, or his nerve, allows him to sit in front of me and inform me of the screenwriting prizes he has won, to tell me that he is a member of the writers unions in the world's most important countries, including the Writers Guild of America West.

I asked him if I could join Argentores, the General Society of Argentine Authors, and his exaggerated laugh echoed throughout the basement.

It was a laugh that was seven laughs at once: seven versions of Santiago, seven different ages laughing at the same time.

He told me that most writers unions in important countries offered him first-rate medical insurance, and that in recent years he had been able to get sick anywhere in the world without paying a cent.

The Writers Guild of America even covers dentists, he told me, thousands of dollars' worth of dentistry. Sometimes, when I'm bored at home upstairs, I think about traveling to the United States, and, a few minutes after landing, yanking out a molar with a pair of pliers, just so I can use some of the money that, if I don't spend it, will surely just be kept by a bunch of people who don't have the slightest idea what writing is.

Santiago promised me that I'd never lack for anything down here, that my basic needs, and others that aren't so basic, would always be met.

If your head hurts, Norma will bring you aspirin, he told me. If your stomach hurts, Buscopan. Fever, ibuprofen. If you have a toothache, Norma will call Dr. Miranda.

Luckily, in the five years I've spent in the basement, I've never had a toothache.

Last year, or the year before that, my gums started to bleed, and Norma brought me these little Gum brand picks with artificial bristles, like tiny brushes (I rub them between my teeth every night), and they eased the swelling in my gums and left them smooth and pink.

Nor do I lack for sun.

The basement has a rectangle of glass bricks that lets in a little sun in the morning.

That rectangle is essential, according to Santiago.

He asks me to sit under the ray of sun for at least an hour a day so I don't end up with a vitamin D deficiency, because the lack of vitamin D lowers your red blood cell count, and that's not something you can fix with pills.

Once a week (Sundays at noon), Norma brings down a vitamin supplement that I swallow with a glass of homemade kombucha.

Norma never speaks to me.

She comes down to the basement three times a day to bring me food, air the place out, make my bed, and clean up a little.

The first few weeks (the following day I woke up in the basement, after that dinner with Santiago when we talked about everything), I tried to start some kind of conversation with Norma, but since she didn't utter a word, or even look at me, I gave up.

Norma is Mexican.

That's what Santiago told me: he brought her here from Mexico.

Though he didn't need to tell me, because from the very first day, Norma has been trying to murder me with her infernal food.

Only a Mexican would cook nearly every dish with *chile poblano* and cilantro.

Since I've been living in the basement, almost all the food I've eaten has been seasoned with *chile poblano* and cilantro.

It took only a few months for the first hemorrhoids to appear.

Santiago offered to call Dr. Miranda.

He offered to have Norma call Dr. Miranda.

But it wasn't necessary.

Santiago told me that he treated his hemorrhoids with some chewable tablets of *ruscus aculeatus*, *bacillus coagulans*, and ascorbic acid.

They're magical, he told me. And I've even had hemorrhoids in my balls.

The pills took effect in less than forty-eight hours.

Now I always keep a blister pack of them beside the mattress, in a Camper shoebox that I call a "nightstand."

Down here you'll never lack for anything, Pablo.

There are so many things I lack.

For example, news about my mother.

Whenever I ask Santiago to please find out how my mother is, he says, "Yes, of course," and then changes the subject.

The next few days, whenever I ask him if he's found out anything about my old lady, he says "Not yet," until I get tired of asking.

Really, it's not that I get tired of asking, it's that Santiago's silence (his non-information about my old lady) makes me think there's only one possibility, and I don't want to think about that possibility; I can't bring myself to ask Santiago about that possibility.

And how are things working out?

Though this may sound ridiculous, I think I've gotten used to life as an imprisoned screenwriter.

No, not imprisoned; *basemented*.

Toward the end of the first year I found a routine that worked, and since then I've kept to it.

As I said before, I write in this notebook from six in the morning to seven in the morning.

Then, from seven in the morning to five after seven, I cross out what I wrote.

Then I pretend to be asleep until Santiago comes down, at seven ten in the morning, with his chair, a cup of coffee, a little dish of fruit, and the printouts of the scenes with his notes.

We work from seven twenty in the morning until one in the afternoon. We fill the blackboard with scribbles that I sometimes have trouble deciphering later.

Then Santiago leaves with his chair, and Norma comes down with lunch.

It only takes me from one ten to one thirty in the afternoon to eat.

Then I take a nap for one hour.

From two thirty in the afternoon until seven thirty at night, I write; sitting on the mattress with my back against the wall, I type on an old 15-inch MacBook Pro whose Wi-Fi, Bluetooth, and Ethernet have been disabled.

I correct the previous scenes based on Santiago's notes (usually, I use about ten percent of his notes), and then I write new scenes based on what Santiago and I discussed (I usually use about thirty percent of his ideas).

At eight at night, Norma comes down with dinner and the external hard drive, and she takes the corrected pages and the new scenes.

It only takes me from eight ten to eight thirty in the evening to eat.

Then I take the two issues of *Playboy* from the nightstand (Santiago changes the magazines three times a year), and I masturbate for at least an hour; I try to make the act of masturbating last as long as possible.

Then, from nine thirty to ten thirty at night, I do nothing.

I look at the ceiling.

Maybe do a push-up or two.

Then Norma comes down to take the tray with the plates and silverware, and to air out the basement; she stands still for a while by the door, letting the oxygen tank renew the foul air.

Sometimes I talk to her, just to bust her balls.

As I said before, I don't try to get a word out of her anymore, I don't try to get her to look at me.

From ten forty-five at night to five fifty in the morning, I sleep.

I sleep quite well in the darkness of the basement.

From six to seven in the morning, I write in this notebook.

Except, ever since Santiago proposed I write the screenplay that has to win everything—ev-er-y-thing—this notebook has been messing with my routine.

It's a constant presence.

Like a hard drug addict who wants to quit but can't get up the nerve to throw away the few grams he has left and instead stashes them away, I hide the notebook during the day and I try to ignore it, but the need to write this and then cross it out ends up overpowering me.

The notebook is now the master of my solitary hours.

*　　*　　*

I'm not sure when I got sick of masturbating.

No, sorry, it's not that I got sick of it (no one gets sick of masturbating), it's just that I started to feel like it wasn't enough.

One morning I mentioned it to Santiago.

He looked at me the way he looks at me when I tell him one of his notes doesn't work, that the scene has to stay how it is, the way I wrote it, in order to be really effective, and that his note, whether it's to add or remove something, will only hurt the scene, that the scene as it is completely fulfills the function it has to fulfill.

Three days later (I think it was a Friday), he came down to the basement with a tall, thin girl with coppery skin, hair black as the basement at night, and green eyes.

He introduced her as Anita.

He told me that, if it was all right with me, Anita would spend a couple of hours in the basement.

It took me no more than half a second to say it was all right with me.

Santiago put a hand on my shoulder, tossed a box of extra-sensitive condoms on the mattress, told me not to be an idiot and to use them, and then he left the basement whistling "Vení Raquel."

Anita stayed still, waiting for me to tell her what to do.

I don't know why I asked her how old she was.

There's nothing worse than asking a woman how old she is, especially when it's the first thing out of your mouth.

Twenty-nine, she said.

In the basement's lousy light I wouldn't have guessed she was over twenty.

I asked her to come closer.

She took a step and then stopped, glancing out of the corner of her eye at the mattress on the floor.

She didn't like that there was no bed, or that the mattress was a twin; she didn't say it, but I could see it in her eyes.

What do you do down here? she asked me.

Her voice didn't match her height and thinness: hers was the voice of a fat girl in whose face someone, some asshole, had screamed "Fat!" at least once a day for many years.

I write, I said.

What do you write?

Movie scripts. Feature films. Dramas. Do you like dramas?

Yes. Not so much. I like comedies better.

Where are you from?

From here.

From San Martín?

No, not from San Martín, from Neuquén. I was born in Zapala.

I sat down on the mattress and gestured for her to sit beside me.

She turned toward the door and then toward me, smiled, took off her sandals, and sat down at the other end of the mattress.

The moment Anita sat down, I realized how horrible the situation was; I understood (or I thought I did) how horrible that situation was for her: locked for two hours in a basement with a stranger, no bed, no windows, no light other than the little ceiling lamp and the one on the nightstand.

I asked her if she wanted something to drink.

She nodded.

I crawled over to the minifridge and opened it: leftover fruit from the morning, a fourth of a bottle of mineral water.

I poured some water into the only glass and handed it to her.

This is all I have, I told her.

Is it mineral water?

Yes, that's the only kind I drink.

She wet her lips, tasting it.

Then she took a sip.

Then she emptied the glass in a long gulp.

Why do you live down here? she asked me.

Santiago didn't tell you?

Who's Santiago?

I took the glass from her and left it on the floor, between the mattress and the wall.

That short conversation with Anita (the fact that she didn't know that the man who brought her to the basement was Santiago Salvatierra, the greatest Latin American film director of all time) reminded me how far removed cinema was for most people—or at least so-called artistic cinema, the kind of film whose sole purpose isn't entertainment.

Something happened in the last few decades that drove most people away from so-called art films.

An invisible wall was gradually built between so-called art films and the majority of the public: those who go to the movies for the sole purpose of being momentarily amused.

In the fifties and sixties, most people went to the movies to amuse themselves watching films by Fellini.

Fellini's films were popular.

These days, most people don't understand Fellini; they don't even know who Fellini is.

A similar thing happened with theater in recent centuries: an invisible wall was gradually built between most people and so-called artistic theater.

In the seventeenth century, most people went to the theater to see Shakespeare's plays.

They laughed and cried and were amused by Shakespeare's plays.

People who didn't know how to read or write.

People who were total philistines.

These days almost no one understands Shakespeare.

Not even the people who believe themselves to be eminently cultured understand Shakespeare.

I don't understand Shakespeare.

Santiago Salvatierra doesn't understand Shakespeare.

The all-time greatest film director in Latin America, and soon in the whole world, doesn't understand Shakespeare.

Writing "Shakespeare" so many times has left me exhausted.

I lay down on the floor, faceup.

I picked a booger that had been stuck for a while to the top of my left nostril.

I tried to remember the lyrics to "Vení Raquel."

Anita put a hand on my thigh; just like that, she rested her left hand on my right thigh and squeezed.

She wanted to say something.

I thought about pouring her some more water.

What's your name? she asked me.

Pablo.

No one should spend so much time in a basement, Pablo. How often do you leave?

I never leave.

Never?

Never.

She took her hand from my thigh.

I thought about telling her my story, starting from that dinner with Santiago when we talked about everything, or even before that, from when I wrote the screenplay about the boy who throws his family into a well.

I should never have written that screenplay.

I should never have sent Santiago that screenplay.

I should never have emailed the screenplay to Santiago's assistant so that she could give it to Santiago.

My friend Lisandro had given me an email address for Santiago's assistant, Patricia.

Lisandro worked as a script supervisor on a Gatorade commercial that Santiago filmed in Buenos Aires.

I don't know how Lisandro, with that face of a frightened rat, managed to seduce Patricia.

I guess he resorted to persistence.

Lisandro was a master of persistence; he was capable of talking to a girl for hours (a girl who'd decided from the very first moment that nothing was going to happen between him and her, never ever), until finally he convinced her to go somewhere else, usually his studio apartment, a room with a single window that looked out onto a brick wall.

So I guess that when he seduced Patricia, he must have resorted to persistence.

They spent almost every night together during the two weeks of the Gatorade shoot.

They declared their undying love for each other.

That's what Lisandro told me.

They arranged to meet up in Cuzco, where Patricia lived in a little house half a block from Santiago's Peruvian mansion.

But Lisandro never went to Cuzco, or even left Buenos Aires as far as I know.

One morning, while I was having breakfast with my old lady—*mate* and Vainillas Capri cookies—Lisandro came to visit.

He couldn't stop smiling.

He took the *mate* gourd and brewed one for himself.

He asked me if I'd finished the screenplay I was writing.

Which one?

The one about the boy who throws his family into a well.

I still hadn't told my old lady I was writing a screenplay about a boy who throws his family into a well, and she looked at me as if she wanted to ask me about that.

I still haven't finished it, I said. I'm missing the third act. I've been stuck on the last twenty pages for a month.

Well, said Lisandro, when you finish it, send a PDF to this email address: ssassistant333@gmail.com.

Why?

Why what?

Why do I have to send a copy of the screenplay about the boy who throws his family into a well to this email address?

Because the email address belongs to Santiago Salvatierra's assistant. Patricia. We're dating. She told me that when you have something you should send it to her, and she'll get it to Santiago.

My old lady asked who this Santiago character was.

An Argentine film director, I told her.

One of the most important directors in the world, said Lisandro.

Not in the world.

Yes, in the world. He's the new Iñárritu. The new Almodóvar. Bigger than Almodóvar. Less queer. Less "Look what a queer I am, and deal with it."

Anita stood up, turned her back to me, and started to get undressed.

Her body was a long, narrow rectangle, not a single curve.

She took off a hairband she wore as a bracelet and pulled her hair into a ponytail.

Before turning around, she asked why I didn't escape:

Why do you agree to live in this basement?

I didn't agree to it, I'm forced to. He kidnapped me.

Now she did turn around, and there was fear in her face, genuine fear.

Are you high? she asked.

No.

Do you drink anything other than mineral water?

Coffee in the morning. A glass of red wine when Santiago comes down at night to tell me about his shitty epiphanies.

She didn't laugh.

Her serious expression scared me.

No, it didn't scare me, it alarmed me profoundly.

I shouldn't have told her everything I told her, I thought. I put her in danger.

Santiago was capable of anything, he'd already proven that.

The first day in the basement, after I'd realized what was happening, after arguing for an hour, after threatening to beat his ass (though I had one arm chained to a pipe whose purpose to this day remains a mystery), I screamed at him that I would not write a word for him, never ever, and he might as well kill me, and Santiago pulled out a gun, a revolver, put a bullet in the chamber and spun it, aimed at me, and pulled the trigger, *click*, and spun the chamber, aimed at me, and pulled the trigger, *click*, and spun the chamber, aimed at me, and pulled the trigger, *click*, until I burst out crying, and Santiago came over and hugged me (the butt of the gun nestled against my back), and he whispered into my ear that together we were going to make art.

The greatest art, Pablo. The only really great art. Because no one makes really great art anymore. *No one.* But you and I are going to. You're going to help me do it. You're going to help me change the world. A world that hasn't changed artistically in decades.

I told Anita that, when she left, if Santiago asked her what we'd talked about for two hours, she should play stupid, pretend she knew nothing.

And how do you know he isn't listening in on us? she asked me. How do you know that computer doesn't have a hidden microphone?

I picked up the laptop, examined it, turned it over, examined it.

The MacBook Pro comes with a built-in microphone, but I doubted Santiago could use it to listen to us.

My old lady told me she thought it was a very good idea.

What is? I asked.

Sending your screenplay to that gentleman, the movie director.

He's not a gentleman, he's almost the same age as me.

Whatever, I think it's a good idea. You never know what might happen. What you do know is, if you don't do anything, then nothing will happen. You don't lose anything by sending it to him.

Nothing's going to come of it.

You've got nothing to lose.

Nothing's going to come of it, Ma.

You've got nothing to lose.

Well, Ma, you were wrong, because I sent the screenplay and I lost my life, both my physical and my intellectual life, my animal and my artistic life.

Sending Santiago the screenplay about the boy who throws his family into a well was the biggest mistake I ever made.

No, the biggest mistake I ever made was accepting Santiago's invitation to spend a weekend at his house in San Martín de los Andes.

Really, if you think about it, it was a series of mistakes, a chain of events that started when I decided to send Santiago (Santiago's assistant) the screenplay about the boy who throws his family into a well, and continued when I accepted Santiago's invitation to spend a weekend at his house in San Martín de los Andes, and it went on continuing when I made the stupid decision not to tell anyone about my trip, not my mother or Lisandro, out of fear I would jinx it, and it continued continuing when, during that dinner with Santiago when we talked about everything, I told him that I hadn't told anyone about the trip out of fear of jinxing it.

I didn't tell him it was out of fear of jinxing it.

The truth is I don't know why I told him I hadn't said a thing to anyone, not about his email congratulating me on the screenplay about the boy who throws his family into a well, not about my upcoming trip to San Martín de los Andes.

Usually, when I meet with someone I consider superior to me (*intellectually* superior, *artistically* superior), I tend to say a lot of unnecessary things.

I can't help it.

Before I meet with someone I consider my superior, I always tell myself that this time I'm not going to say anything unnecessary, I'm not going to ramble; I swear it to myself, right hand over my heart, and then, after a few minutes sitting across from the person I consider superior to me, the first unnecessary sentence escapes me, and a little while later the second, and after that there's no stopping me.

I leave my body and watch myself speak.

I see myself saying things I don't want to say, things there's no need for me to say.

*   *   *

Santiago just left.

He's worried.

Another one of his skeptical nights.

It happens at least once a month.

Suddenly he thinks everything is wrong, he wants to rewrite it all.

I asked him to calm down.

I told him the best thing for him is to let a few days go by and then read the screenplay again, and not make any rushed decisions.

No, there's nothing for it, he wants to trash it all.

He walks in circles, his right hand brushing the basement walls.

He walks in rectangles.

He moved the mattress away from the wall so he could walk in rectangles.

Three forty in the morning.

I read him one of the scenes I worked on yesterday, and he looked at me with hatred.

Santiago is capable of hating me intensely on his skeptical nights; I could read him a scene from Edward Albee, tell him it was mine, and he'd look at me and ask where the hell I ever got the idea to be a writer when it's clear I don't have an ounce of talent.

And then, after laying into me for a while, he usually lashes out against everyone who ever worked for him (the actors, directors of photography, art directors, soundtrack composers, editors, etc.), and he asks someone who is not in the basement with us why the hell he always has to put up with such a band of imbeciles, why does he always have to be the one who kills himself working in order to save the films from the depths of mediocrity into which everyone who works for him keeps trying to push them?

Santiago has cultivated a talent for off-loading responsibility onto others.

Only very occasionally is he hit with an acute attack of what he calls "self-loathing."

He told me: I can spend two or three days brooding around the house, avoiding my reflection in the mirror, any mirror, because if I see myself, even if it's just out of the corner of my eye, there's a risk I will charge toward my reflection and hurt myself. Beating the living daylights out of myself. A pretty odd expression, now that I think about it: beating the living daylights out of someone. Daylight, after all, isn't living. And even if you can make the argument that it is living, daylight's not inside a person. And even if daylight were inside a person, how could you beat it out?

Anita asked me if I wanted to do something.

My old lady asked me if she could read the screenplay about the boy who throws his family into a well.

I'm still not finished, Ma. When I finish it I'll give you a copy.

I never gave her a copy.

No one read the screenplay about the boy who threw his family into a well, except for Santiago, and his assistant, I guess.

A screenplay I never should have written.

A screenplay that will never be produced.

A screenplay that is without a doubt the best thing I've written.

Anita asked me if I wanted to kiss her.

I told her I did.

She made it clear that if I kissed her it was going to cost more.

That's okay, I said, I'm not the one paying for it.

I took her by the hand and pulled her back down to the mattress.

I caressed her face.

We kissed.

A simple kiss, lips against lips, no tongue.

A simple, un-erotic kiss that sent a shock through me.

I felt my body expand.

Another shock went through me, and it made my stomach turn.

I had to get away, walk to the minifridge, take a sip of water.

The water was a mistake.

Too late I remembered my old lady saying it was a good idea to drink water before you stick your fingers down your throat to vomit, because water provokes retching.

I closed my eyes, trying not to think about the only thing I was able to think about: Norma's chicken mole with rice rotting in my stomach.

I rushed to the bathroom and knelt before the toilet.

The bathroom is the size of a coffin.

The water in the shower falls directly onto the toilet and the sink.

There's no bidet.

I use a portable bidet: a little squeezable plastic bottle with a mini-shower head on the end.

It was one of the few conditions I gave Santiago after the revolver incident: I told him that if he didn't resolve the issue of the bidet, it would be impossible for me to live in the basement.

I don't know how eighty percent of the world manages to live without a bidet.

Eighty percent?

Sixty?

The sight of the chicken mole with rice in the toilet water turned my stomach again, but there was nothing left to throw up.

I flushed.

I considered wiping myself off with Borges's *Complete Works.*

I keep the three volumes in the medicine cabinet, alongside the toothbrush, toothpaste, and deodorant.

I don't want to see them while I'm writing.

I don't want to have them near me.

Santiago is obsessed with Borges; Borges is the only artist, other than Tarkovsky, whom he truly admires.

My first week in the basement he brought me his copy of the *Complete Works: Critical Edition*, published by Grupo Planeta.

He told me that Borges is, in his opinion, the greatest writer to ever exist; that Borges is Homer, Schopenhauer, Dickens, and Dostoyevsky all rolled into one.

He told me that part of the reason he had invited me to work with him was because, like him, I'm Argentine, and Argentina is the only Latin American country to produce real writers.

He told me that the towering writers from literary countries like Mexico, Chile, and Colombia are midgets compared to the great Argentine writers, that they can't even reach their Argentine ankles, that Rulfo and Neruda and García Márquez can't even scratch the soles of Borges's or Cortázar's feet.

Though then he added that even Cortázar himself couldn't reach the soles of Borges's feet, not even with the very tips of his fingers.

I felt a little sick at the thought of Borges's feet, but I didn't say anything.

During those first few weeks I tried not to contradict Santiago very much.

That's why I didn't tell him, either, about my inability to read Borges.

I waited over a year to tell Santiago I couldn't read Borges.

Between the ages of twenty-seven and twenty-nine, I adored Borges's prose more than anything in the world.

It was the only thing I read.

Not the only thing, but whenever I read anything that wasn't Borges, I compared it to Borges, and ended up putting the book down after just a few pages.

Between the ages of twenty-seven and twenty-nine, I was trapped in Borges's prose, imprisoned in his *Complete Works.*

I had bought the three volumes with money I found in one of the pockets of my old man's favorite jacket after he died, his neck snapped by the airplane.

I would carry one of those four volumes with me everywhere.

Especially Volume I.

I would walk around Buenos Aires with Volume I of Borges's *Complete Works* tucked under my arm.

Until one day I sat down on a bench in the highest part of Barrancas de Belgrano to read Borges and eat a hot dog with mustard and ketchup, and when I moved my eyes over the first paragraph of "The Circular Ruins," I felt that each and every one of the words was gratuitous.

Suddenly I was overcome by the artificiality of Borges's prose, and ever since then I haven't been able to read him, not even the essays or the most minimalist stories of Volume III.

The worst thing about Borges is his use of words; the best things about Borges are his intelligence and humor.

Borges wrote prose that was too infatuated with the word.

Which is what I told Santiago one day before he picked up his chair and left the basement.

He looked at me like he wanted to slap me.

And who the fuck do you think you are? Where's the great prose you write? What phrase have you written that gets anywhere near "A lean and evil mob of moon-colored hounds breaks out from behind the black rosebushes"?

I tried to explain to him that, maybe, my problem with Borges was (is) that I had overdone it with Borges, that I had allowed Borges to negate the rest of my life—all that was life and that did not exist in his *Collected Works*.

I'm not about to take Borges out of here, Pablo, he told me. Those books are yours. You keep them. Read them if you want to, if you don't want to, don't. But I recommend you read them.

I don't read them.

I never read them.

It makes no sense to read them.

Because Borges's *Complete Works*, if you read them seriously, will only ruin you.

Santiago is ruined as a writer, not only because he can't write, but also because he reads Borges incessantly.

Borges ruined Santiago, just as he ruined many others.

The great writers of history do nothing but ruin us.

We can't escape them, we can only be ruined by them.

Anita asked me if I was all right.

I rinsed my mouth, gargled dramatically several times, and apologized.

It's not your fault, I said. It has nothing to do with you. It's just that it's been a long time since . . .

I understand, she said.

I saw in her eyes that she did understand, not that I really knew what there was to understand.

I lay down faceup on the mattress.

Anita had gone to the door, placed her hand on the doorknob, but she didn't turn it.

Instead, she went into the bathroom.

Silence.

I asked her what she was doing.

She didn't answer.

I heard the faucet turn on and off, less than a second of water hitting the sink.

Then she came out of the bathroom, came over to me, asked me to move over, and lay down beside me, her breasts resting against my left arm.

We stayed like that for a long time.

Then I heard Anita whisper something into my ear, I didn't quite catch what.

I said yes anyway.

I turned to look at her.

We kissed again.

She took off her panties and I lowered my sweatpants to my ankles.

She slipped the condom on me with admirable ease, never taking her eyes from mine.

When I penetrated her, I was overcome by a freezing, sticky cold, like dry ice.

My heart was trying to warn me of something.

I didn't even last five minutes.

Anita got dressed slowly; the clothing hung from her body like it had been set out to dry on the back of a chair.

I never saw her again.

One morning I asked Santiago about Anita.

Anita?

The girl you brought last Friday.

Oh, right, Anita. What a stupid name. She didn't want to come back. She said she didn't like you. She has plenty of clients, and she didn't like you.

*   *   *

Today we really dove into the second act.

Santiago came downstairs with his chair, the cup of coffee, and the little dish of fruit, and we spent two hours discussing the three-act Aristotelian diagram, setting the key plot points, as well as each point's action, conflict, and twist.

It's going well.

My brain hurts, which is a good sign.

While he scrawls on the blackboard, Santiago eats dark chocolate with sea salt; four or five bars per session.

Every now and then he offers me a square, and I refuse, explaining for the millionth time that chocolate gives me a headache, and he nods, and after a while he offers me another square.

The first act works: it introduces the protagonists and the main conflict, all with a degree of surprise, a bit of misdirection, but never veering into the absurd.

Santiago hates the absurd; he thinks it's gratuitous, anti-artistic.

He has to construct what he calls a "common sense box," a box in which there's a connection between the film's world and the real world, and then he tries to fly inside that box.

He never breaks out of the box.

He won't allow any free association or crazy impulse to remove him from the box.

The second act is always the hardest.

Not because it's the longest; no, the fact that it's long makes it a little easier. If the second act were as short as the first it would be impossible to write.

The second act (at least it was the second act the last two times) is where Santiago and I bang our heads against the wall: I grab his head with both hands and smash it against the wall, and he grabs my head in both hands and smashes mine against the wall.

In the second act, there's blood.

The second act is the battle that defines the war.

Many's the screenplay I abandoned in the second act.

A second act has left me in the dust more than once.

I wonder if any of Peter Shaffer's second acts ever left him in the dust.

The second act of *Amadeus* is one of the best second acts ever written.

It ends when Salieri finally understands (that is, succumbs to the idea) that God has been laughing at him his entire life; that the pact between them (a pact that meant everything to Salieri—he never touched a woman out of respect for the pact) meant nothing to God.

Suddenly, Salieri's world loses all order and descends into chaos.

A plot point usually called "All Is Lost."

The three-act structure usually has five main plot points: the beginning, the end of the first act, the halfway point that divides the second act in two, the end of the second act, and the resolution.

The word that we're using to identify the starting point of the Aristotelian diagram for this third screenplay, the one that's supposed to change the course of world cinema history, is "Infestation," in English. Not *infestación*, not *plaga*.

We write our scripts in Spanish—I don't know why Santiago likes to use English words to identify the plot points.

The word that identifies the end of the first act is "Tree."

Now we have to build the scenes that get us from "Tree" to the middle point that cuts the second act in two, a plot point that, after several weeks of discussion, we have identified with the word "Adoption."

It usually takes us around six months to finish the second act.

It's an interminable exercise of trial and error.

The fact that we have the story all thought out, planned, and diagrammed, doesn't mean that during the writing process we won't find doors that close and lock us out.

The purpose of the work that comes before the writing, the many months spent plotting the story, is to build the box.

A box custom-made for what Santiago wants.

A box that contains the subject, the tone, and the key plot points.

A box that contains the protagonists' backstories and their Aristotelian framework.

Then, when it comes time to start writing, I get inside the box, put both feet into it, and I discover, as if for the first time, that there's a lot of room in there, and the box holds many paths that can be taken.

That same carefully designed box contains an infinite number of films.

That same box can give birth to a horrible film, a mediocre film, an insignificant film, an acceptable film, a good film, an interesting film, a very good film, an almost excellent film, an excellent film, or a work of art, the sort that walks up to film history and punches it in the nose.

A box that, though it doesn't physically exist, I can see.

ENCRYPTED WORD FILE

Santiago found the notebook.

He asked me what the notebook is, what it means.

I asked him how he'd found it.

He told me it didn't matter how he'd found it, the important thing was that he'd found it, and now he wanted to know what it was, what it meant.

Nothing, I told him. Notes. Shit I write at night.

Why do you cross it out?

Because it's bullshit.

If it was bullshit you wouldn't cross it out. There's no need to cross out bullshit.

I didn't know what to say.

We looked at each other.

Santiago looked like he wanted to give me a good slap.

He'd tried to read what I'd written through the marks, but couldn't.

I'd crossed out the words in the notebook so carefully, using black ink to completely cover the blue ink, that it was impossible to read them.

He took the notebook away anyway.

I'm typing this in an encrypted Word file that I save in a folder hidden deep in this 15-inch laptop.

Today I have to write the first scene of the second act.

I couldn't sleep, thinking about that scene.

An uncontrollable anxiety is making my heart pound, and I keep having to check my pulse.

I don't know what this scene is.

I know what the scene has to be, what happens in the scene, how it starts and ends, but I don't know what it *is*.

I tried to keep going without the notebook, to ignore my need for the notebook, but ultimately I opened this Word file, and now every time I get stuck on a scene I'm going to be tempted to write in this Word file.

I need to learn some kind of encryption that takes several minutes (at least fifteen, or half an hour) to unencrypt; a kind of encryption that I'm too lazy to unencrypt, except when I feel the overwhelming need to go on writing in this file.

A password that takes me fifteen minutes to type.

A gigantic word.

How many characters can you use as an encryption password in Word files?

It pisses me off to not have internet.

It pisses me off not to know how Santiago managed to find the notebook.

When did he find it?

I never leave.

While I was showering?

Maybe Norma saw it while she was cleaning.

But what did she see?

What's the difference between the notebook and the dictionary of the Spanish Royal Academy, the Longman Spanish–English dictionary, the *Complete Works* of Borges?

It's all in the same pile of books.

It's all material I use for work.

Except for Borges's *Complete Works*.

What did Norma see in the notebook that caught her attention?

The crossed-out lines?

There's nothing strange in crossing things out.

Crossing things out is part of writing, an essential part.

Santiago never saw the notebook, not that I know of, not in all the thousands of hours we spent working.

I brought that notebook with me from Buenos Aires.

Now that I think about it, I used that notebook during that first dinner with Santiago when we talked about everything, to write down a list of the films he wanted me to see.

La dolce vita.

Stalker.

Seven Samurai.

Songs from the Second Floor.

El Topo.

2001: A Space Odyssey.

Sunrise: A Song of Two Humans.

Bicycle Thieves.

Fitzcarraldo.

La dolce vita.

During that first dinner with Santiago when we talked about everything, I never imagined I would end up watching those films locked in a basement.

Santiago came down one morning with his 75-inch TV and his Blu-ray player, asked Norma to make a jug of coffee, another of skim milk (for me), another of almond milk (for him), another of orange juice, and a plate of Lincoln and Sonrisas cookies, and we sat down to watch all those movies in the order he listed them, starting and ending with *La dolce vita*.

After the credits for the second *La dolce vita* finished rolling (Santiago likes to watch movies from the colored bars until the very end, meaning that he sat there reading, or pretending to read, the full list of credits for all the films we watched together in the basement), I asked him if he'd like to watch *Amadeus*, since it was one of my favorite movies.

He looked at me the way he looks at me when I say something he doesn't agree with, and he told me that Miloš Forman, in his opinion, was a lesser director.

A good director, don't get me wrong, but lesser, he said. A run-of-the-mill director. A good run-of-the-mill director. What I mean is, when it comes to milled directors, Miloš Forman is at the top, along with Kusturica, Polanski, Tarantino. A great guy, Miloš Forman. He had me over for breakfast at his house in Čáslav.

Čáslav?

In Czechoslovakia. A beautiful little town. There's not shit to do there, but it's lovely. A great guy, Miloš Forman.

One morning during my second year in the basement (if I remember correctly we were working on the third act of the first screenplay we wrote together—or rather, that I wrote for him and he put only his name on), Santiago came down with his 75-inch TV and his Blu-ray player and he made me watch all of his films, the ones he directed.

I had already seen most of them, but he made me watch them anyway.

He commented on small details from every single scene we watched, like a tailor-made commentary track, live and in person.

He explained how he had struggled with several of the actors to achieve the result he was looking for, the maximum possible perfection.

He told me, laughing, that he'd threatened to murder several of those actors; he'd even threatened to make one of their mothers disappear.

I hired extras to act as paid assassins, he told me, and I told them to keep quiet and stand near the video assist with the butt of a prop gun peeking out from under their black jackets. Black jackets and black shirts and black pants and black shoes. All black. Threatening. And the actors trembled. I swear. I saw them trembling, and I heard them say things like "We'd better not fuck up," or "Get it together, this shit's for real." I always leave the microphones on and I hear what they say. Even when they go to the bathroom. I hear how hard they flush the toilet. That's important: how hard they flush the toilet.

Santiago gestures inordinately when he talks: he speaks with his mouth and also with his hands.

He went bald young, before he turned thirty, and now he shaves his head and his beard with a razor every morning.

He told me Norma holds up a little mirror to help him shave the nape of his neck.

Santiago has a prominent nose; not immense like mine, but prominent, a nose that tries to escape his face.

He lives in constant torment from the hairs sprouting from his nostrils.

Every few minutes he runs his fingers over his nostrils, and if he finds a stray hair, he stuffs it back in.

I no longer shave or trim the hairs in my nostrils or ears.

Norma cuts my hair every once in a while, violently, with a pair of those scissors they give to kids to cut paper when they make collages.

Scissors that yank out my hair more than cut it.

Scissors that wouldn't be very useful if I ever got the idea to grab them from Norma and threaten to stab her with them, because they aren't pointed.

My beard is down to my belly button.

One night when I was bored, I asked Norma to find me a ruler and I measured it: 55.8 centimeters.

By now it must be past 60.

I guess.

I never measured it again.

The hairs in my ears grow out angry and tangled.

Sometimes I rub them.

Sometimes I let out farts that take half an hour to go away.

The basement's ventilation leaves a lot to be desired; just good enough so I don't faint on a regular basis.

Or maybe I do faint.

Maybe that's how Santiago found the notebook: they come into the basement when I faint.

No, I'm sure I would realize if I were about to faint, I would feel something, some kind of dizziness.

Not that I know how a person feels when they're about to run out of air.

Santiago looks like he's about to faint every time I mention Michael Haneke.

In my opinion, Haneke is the greatest film director of the past three decades.

And Santiago knows I'm right.

I'm sure he knows, and that's why he avoids mentioning his name, and also why every time I mention Haneke, Santiago looks like he's about to faint and then he changes the subject.

I remember we talked about Haneke on my first night in San Martín de los Andes.

We were discussing the suicide of one of the characters in Santiago's last film (the last one he cowrote with his Spanish partner, Fermín Hermida), and I mentioned *The Seventh Continent*, my favorite Haneke film, the best film ever made about suicide.

Santiago's expression changed when I uttered the Austrian's name: his outsized enthusiasm shrank, recoiled.

He told me that *The Seventh Continent* was a good film, without a doubt a good film, but it was also a failed film.

It's a film that is nothing but a question, he said, one long question, a mystery, if you like, that at the end is answered. That's all it is: one long question that is answered in the end. There is no empathy. The characters don't change, they don't improve or get worse. One suffers a little for the girl, it's true, and what a good actress that little girl is, but not for the parents. The parents die, they kill the girl and then they kill themselves, and you think: "Okay, that happened, that family decided to abandon the world, and now, what's for dinner?"

In the second act of this third screenplay, there's a suicide.

A suicide that, if it's well acted (there's no doubt it will be well directed, well lit, and have just the right soundtrack), could be one of the most powerful suicides in film history.

A completely surprising suicide that at the same time is inevitable.

A suicide that everyone will see coming, or almost everyone, and that at the same time everyone, or almost everyone, will watch with the utmost surprise.

A suicide that viewers are going to take home with them, that Santiago Salvatierra fans are going to frame and hang up on the walls of their living or dining rooms.

A suicide that will be stamped onto the bestselling T-shirt ever.

A suicide so fascinating, if I manage to write it well, that it terrifies me.

I'm terrified by the temptation to imitate that suicide.

Today in bed, while I ate the last bits of pineapple that I saved from breakfast, I had the thought that the only way to write that suicide is by imitating it.

*   *   *

I asked Santiago to get me a guitar.

Any guitar.

Acoustic.

Classical.

A cheap one.

After a few hours he came down with a Blackbird tenor ukelele, brand-new, made in the United States and entirely of carbon fiber.

An instrument like that must cost a fortune.

I asked him how he managed to find a carbon fiber ukelele in San Martín de los Andes, and he told me that one of his neighbors is Gustavo Santaolalla, the musician, that they're friends and Santiago asked him for a guitar, but apparently Santaolalla didn't have any guitars to lend out—he needs all his guitars—and he only had this Blackbird ukelele that he'd bought on a whim at a music store in San Francisco and has barely ever used.

The ukelele sounds almost like a guitar.

The acoustics in the basement are perfect: my own personal Teatro Colón.

Tomorrow I'm going to ask Santiago to get me an exercise book for ukelele learners.

I'm also going to ask for Beatles sheet music.

The Beatles are the only thing I listen to; I have their entire discography on the laptop.

An understanding of the Beatles was the best thing I got out of my two years of music school.

I became a Beatles addict.

They're all I listened to before I came to San Martín de los Andes, and they're all I listen to in the basement.

It was one of the first things I asked Santiago for, after the bidet, after asking him to solve my bidet problem.

When I found out he was going to lend me (lend, not give) a 15-inch MacBook Pro to work on, I asked him to copy all the Beatles' albums onto a USB drive, including the BBC sessions.

That same night, Santiago took the laptop and bought every one of the Beatles' albums on iTunes, along with several albums by Lennon, McCartney, and Harrison, and he gave the Beatle-loaded laptop back to me the next morning over breakfast.

Santiago hates piracy.

If I even come close to suggesting that he download something from the internet, some PDF of a book we need for what we're writing or some album that could perhaps serve as inspiration for a future soundtrack, he looks at me the way he does when I say something he doesn't like, and he clarifies that he will buy the album on iTunes that evening, or he asks me to wait a few days so he can have the book we need sent to him by Librería Norte.

All the books that Santiago buys, he buys from Librería Norte.

According to Santiago, it's the only worthwhile bookstore in Buenos Aires:

When Librería Norte goes under—and I pray to God that never happens—Buenos Aires won't be worth a damn. Nothing in Buenos Aires matters besides Librería Norte. The museums and galleries are pathetic. The old movie theaters are falling apart, and the new chain theaters project in digital, which robs them of all value as theaters.

The chain bookstores offer next to nothing, copious quantities of next to nothing. There are some new, small bookstores in neighborhoods like Palermo or Barracas, but they don't have much to offer, and the little they do have runs out soon enough. All we have left is Librería Norte. An entire city depends on that bookstore not disappearing.

I told him that I used to go to Librería Norte a lot, that I'd discovered several of my favorite writers there.

I discovered Beckett there, and Joyce, Laiseca, DeLillo, Flannery O'Connor.

I discovered Arno Schmidt there.

At Librería Norte I read Philip Larkin for the first time, and Philip Roth and David Markson.

Santiago has never read Markson.

He's barely read Beckett.

Santiago hates Beckett with all his soul; he's one of those people who can't read Beckett, who can't even look at him, one of those people whose stomach turns at the mere thought of Beckett.

It was at Librería Norte that I saw Lisandro for the last time, when I went with him to buy the Cátedra edition of Joyce's *Ulysses*.

We met at the Frattempo bar, on Pueyrredón and Peña; we drank hot chocolate and shared a ham and cheese sandwich.

If I remember correctly, we talked about Patricia, Santiago's assistant.

Lisandro didn't know what to do about Patricia.

He told me that he liked her, liked her a lot, but she didn't turn him on in the slightest.

The most fucked-up part about it is that I don't know why she doesn't turn me on, he told me. She has all the things necessary to turn me on, but I don't get turned on. When I'm in bed with her, I have to think about one of the women I saw that day in the street or online. I have to close my eyes and imagine that this woman with me, naked, is not Patricia but some woman from Russia or Poland or Japan.

I asked him if he was going to break up with her.

Hell no, he said.

Then we walked to Librería Norte.

They didn't have copies of the Cátedra edition of *Ulysses*, so Lisandro ordered it.

We left, he told me he had to be somewhere, and we clapped one another on the shoulder.

Today I ate my breakfast thinking about Lisandro.

What ever happened to my friend?

While Santiago explained how he planned to film one of the first scenes in the second act, I tried to imagine what had become of my friend's life.

I thought about asking Santiago to get me some information about Lisandro, so I'd at least know he was alive.

But no, most likely Santiago would say, "Yeah, sure thing," and then do nothing.

Maybe he would do it for my own good.

That is, do nothing for my own good.

I'm fine like this, not knowing what's become of Lisandro or my mother.

I imagine Lisandro trying to finish his business administration degree, a degree he'd started in order to pacify his parents and that after more than ten years he still couldn't finish.

I imagine my old lady coordinating the children's party shows; waging war and later becoming friends with Mrs. Wasserman, who made the costumes of superheroes and princesses and Disney characters; having her breakfast *mate* every morning with La Merced brand, at that hour when the first sun ruins the night: in summer at five thirty in the morning, in winter at six thirty.

I used to like to wake to the sounds of my mother in the kitchen, and then go on sleeping for a few more hours, knowing she was there, with her *mate*, watching the sunrise.

It's been five years since I've seen a sunrise.

Five years since I've seen a tree.

Five years since I've seen a cloud.

And to think that I'm in one of the prettiest towns in Argentina, one of the most picturesque.

I still remember how that landscape dazzled me the morning I landed, when Santiago brought me in his four-by-four truck from the Chapelco Airport to his house.

The myriad colors of nature.

The endless blue of the sky.

The smell of pure air, so different from the air in Buenos Aires.

Here in the basement everything ends, there's no such thing as endless, there's no myriad of anything.

The rectangle of light obscures what's on the other side.

It lights up and goes dark, lights up and goes dark.

And the air . . .

I already talked about the air.

Talked?

Who am I talking to?

My mother?

Lisandro?

Peter Shaffer?

I'm going to ask Santiago to find out if Peter Shaffer is alive.

What difference does it make?

Peter Shaffer doesn't matter anymore.

No one who has ever written anything matters anymore.

All that matters are the scenes I write for Santiago.

And this encrypted file.

And Santaolalla's ukelele.

And the Beatles albums.

I never listen to the solo albums by Lennon, McCartney, or Harrison, I only listen to the Beatles.

That band is a clear example of the virtues of collaboration.

A band made up of four very talented musicians who, when they got together, transformed that talent into genius; they stopped being themselves, left behind the talented individual musicians in order to become part of something great, something bigger than what they were individually.

Luckily Santiago lent me his Bose headphones—it would be very sad to listen to the Beatles on the laptop's built-in speakers.

The sound comes out of the keyboard.

A speaker made of keys.

A speaker that is ruining the younger generation's auditory perception.

Santiago told me that upstairs in his house he has a surround sound system: dozens of little speakers, hidden in the ceiling and walls of his studio, that take the music apart and reconstruct in the air just before it reaches his ears.

One hour a day, at least, I sit in my leather armchair and listen to history's great composers, he told me. I let them enter me, elevate me, lift me out of this degenerate world for a while. I am filled with the notes of the great composers, I inflate like a balloon, and I float. I let myself be carried along like a lost balloon, a balloon adrift.

Santiago can be really cheesy.

The greatest Latin American film director of all time is addicted to platitudes and cheese.

Maybe that's why he's the greatest.

Maybe mixing genius with cheesiness and platitudes is essential to being the greatest.

Haneke completely lacks cheesiness and platitudes.

Maybe that's why, though to me he is the greatest, and to Santiago, too (though he won't admit it), the world can't accept Haneke as its greatest director.

Though now that I think of it, in one of his most recent movies, *Amour* (Santiago and I watched it here in the basement), Haneke did play around with some platitudes.

I don't know about cheesiness, but definitely platitudes.

And *Amour* won that year's Oscar for Best Foreign Language Film.

That's what Santiago told me: that after hitting the goalpost with *The White Ribbon*, Haneke scored a corner goal with *Amour*.

And it's likely that part of what made *Amour* fly over the goalie and into that corner was the use of a few platitudes.

Haneke had to recur to platitudes in order to be that year's best non-American director.

You can't be the greatest director with a film like *The Seventh Continent*, or with *71 Fragments of a Chronology of Chance*.

Those movies are too good.

Such good movies will never make a director into the greatest.

*   *   *

Santiago is stuck on the final twist in the third scene of the second act: he's unconvinced.

The twist is a door that opens unexpectedly at the end of the scene.

Any scene that is not a transition must have a twist.

Action, conflict, and twist, or what's also referred to as "scene reversal."

One of the characters carries the action, wants something, needs something.

The conflict is what comes between the character and that something.

Whether the character has obtained the something or not, the twist is what pushes him someplace unexpected.

For example, in *Amadeus* there is a scene where Mozart's wife brings her husband's compositions to Salieri in the hopes that the maestro will recognize Mozart's talent and offer him work.

The action is the woman's, she needs her husband to find work, a commission, anything—she needs money.

The conflict is that she doesn't know that Salieri detests Mozart.

That is, he detests God for having put Mozart in his path, but by extension he detests Mozart.

And the thing that aggravates the conflict is what Salieri finds in those scores: genius, once again!

But not only that—the scores are originals. The woman didn't bring copies, she brought the originals, and they have no corrections.

This provokes in Salieri (in F. Murray Abraham) one of the most perfect expressions ever captured on film.

An expression impossible to understand.

An expression that should terrify all other actors in the world, make them consider retiring, or leaping from the stage and fleeing.

The twist is Salieri's silent exit.

After he is overcome by Mozart's genius, the sheets of music fall to the floor, and Mozart's wife asks, "Is it not good?" and Salieri replies, "It is miraculous," and she smiles and bends over to pick up the scores, and she asks him, "So you will help us?" and Salieri, without a word, leaves the room.

A subtle twist, but enough to leave us a little lost.

What is happening inside Salieri?

What is he going to do, against Mozart or against God?

Leaving the viewer a little lost is good.

A little, not entirely.

When the viewer is entirely lost, he falls out of the film.

Santiago thinks there are several possible reversals for each scene, and he always plays with various possibilities, but he is wrong: if the scene is well constructed, there is only one possible reversal.

That's why it takes me so long to finish the scenes, and that's why it pisses me off when Santiago comes downstairs to question the twist and to propose others, always worse, always inadequate.

Each scene is like a Beatles song.

A song that arises from collaboration, that couldn't exist without collaboration, but that depends on one single composer who determines the details.

The Beatles had an understanding that for each song, one of them would take the lead, and they respected that understanding.

Lennon took the lead when it was one of his songs, he told the others what to do, what to play, and the others tossed out ideas that ended up improving the song, but they respected Lennon's final decision.

Then, when they gave a song to McCartney, Lennon strapped on his guitar and stood aside, and he let McCartney take the lead.

Santiago is convinced that he takes the lead in every one of our scenes, that all the scenes are ultimately his compositions and that what I do is collaborate with him, help him make his scenes better.

Santiago is convinced that he is Lennon and McCartney, and I am Harrison.

No, he is Lennon, McCartney, and Harrison, and I'm Ringo Starr.

Which if it were true wouldn't bother me in the slightest; I have enormous respect for Ringo's work with the Beatles. An uneducated, self-taught drummer, but one who precisely for that reason is creative and difficult, at his best moments, to imitate.

I wouldn't have any problem being Ringo, I would be more than proud, if that were reality.

But the reality is that Santiago, when it comes to writing screenplays, is no Lennon or McCartney or Harrison or Ringo.

Santiago is Yoko Ono.

Yoko spent all her time in the studio, gave opinions, said a thousand things a minute, no one listened to her, or almost no one, and then she went away convinced she was an essential part of the Beatles.

Santiago is Yoko Ono, pregnant in a bed in the recording studio, under the sheets with a microphone that she uses to bust everyone's balls.

It took me over two hours to convince him that the twist I used in the scene is the right one.

We left it as it was.

He told me that the actors he plans to use for this third film (he still hasn't told me their names) are free from March to August next year.

You have to hurry up, Pablo, he told me. I don't want to rush you. I don't want you to write in a rush. But you do have to hurry.

It's not long until March: three and a half months.

A hundred and five days to get the shooting draft ready.

That means I have to finish the first draft in two months.

Then we'll take one month more to polish it and get the second draft ready, and fifteen days for the shooting draft.

Santiago says that, really, he can start preproduction with the first draft.

I have a month and a half to write the second act, and fifteen days for the third.

There it is again: my tachycardia.

The certainty I'm going to have a heart attack.

I played it cool, but I couldn't keep myself from checking my pulse in my left wrist with the index and middle finger of my right hand.

Santiago saw me but didn't say anything.

He asked me if I wanted barbecue for dinner tonight.

Sure, I said.

I'm going to throw a filet and a skirt steak on the grill. What kind of sausage do you like?

Chinchulín, chorizo. Anything but tripe.

He sat for a while looking at me, and his eyes held an intention to say something more.

In hindsight, I think he wanted to invite me to eat barbecue with him upstairs, in his house, that for a moment he was considering inviting me up to eat with him.

I've just dipped the last piece of baguette in the juice.

My old lady is disgusted by meat juice, which she mistakenly calls "blood."

When we went to barbecues, she would ask for her filet butter-flied and well done. Two shoe soles that smelled of burnt charcoal.

I hope she is still going to barbecues and asking for shoe soles.

I hope she has met someone who takes her to barbecues to enjoy her shoe soles with tossed salad.

My routine has gone to hell.

I've just finished dinner and I'm already writing in this encrypted file.

"A Day in the Life."

There is nothing more gratifying, musically speaking, than listening to the album *Sgt. Pepper's Lonely Hearts Club Band* through headphones.

Though I've listened to this album a thousand times, the sound design never ceases to surprise me: instruments and voices that jump unexpectedly from left to right, right to left; instruments and voices that awaken unexpectedly in my ears and fill my head.

The arrangements are at once minimalist and extravagant.

George Martin had a grand old time playing with those four kids: his puppets, his prehistoric GarageBand.

How excited he must have been when he arrived at the studio, wondering what they would turn up with that day, knowing he would be able to play with whatever it was the four Liverpudlians brought him.

*   *   *

I can hear the rain.

It's pouring.

Only once has the power gone out in the basement.

It took Santiago three hours to come down with a flashlight.

He told me not to worry, he'd already ordered a generator and it would be here in a few days.

Most likely the electricity has gone out other times (there've been other downpours), but the generator covered the lack of electricity.

Although I would have realized if the electricity went out, because it would take a few minutes to get the generator going.

I guess.

I imagine the entire town of San Martín de los Andes without electricity, except for Santiago Salvatierra's house.

A house lit up in the middle of the most absolute darkness.

A house that is the only house in the world.

The house where the history of world cinema is being changed.

Four twenty in the morning.

Santiago has just left.

He came down drunk.

He'd downed three bottles of Prosecco with a piece of meat left over from yesterday.

He brought one of the Oscars down with him, the most recent one for Best Foreign Film.

He apologized for not having shown it to me sooner.

I'll leave it here if you want, he said. You can put it there, next to the mattress, and look at it when you go to bed.

No, thanks. I'm okay.

Of course you're okay. Why wouldn't you be okay? You don't need this Oscar. No one needs this Oscar. Best Foreign Film. What does that mean?

It means—

Nothing. It means nothing. An Oscar doesn't mean shit. Use it as a paperweight. I have another one upstairs. Another Oscar. And that one doesn't mean shit, either. I'm going to go get it for you. You can keep them both.

No, thanks, I don't want them.

Why not?

Because I don't. They're yours.

I know they're mine. But you can borrow them. Best Foreign Film.

He hugged me.

It's the second time he's hugged me, and the only time after that first day with the revolver.

This time, instead of the gun butt against my back, I feel the Oscar; the base of the Oscar where they screw in the golden plaque with the name of the film and the director, or screenwriter, or costume designer, or editor, or . . .

He lay down on the mattress and covered his face with his hands.

He told me his ex-wife is getting married next month.

She sent me an invitation, he said. Can you believe it? That shameless bitch sent me an invitation. She's marrying one of those dummies who develop cell phone applications. He struck it rich with one that tells you how many colors are in the food you eat in a week. What variety of colors you eat. Apparently it's important to vary the colors of your food. Millions, he made. They're getting married on the beach, in front of their house in Punta del Este. His house, which will soon be hers. And Hilario's. Hilario is going to live with them. Didn't I tell you? He let me know last week. He sent me an email. My son communicates with me by email. He doesn't call anymore, or if he does call it's to ask for cash. Emails with no punctuation, incorrect spelling, bad grammar. He doesn't get a single word right.

He sat up on the mattress and looked at me with absurd seriousness:

We have to kick some ass, Pablo. There can be no doubt. I've already gotten an American translator, one of the good ones, the woman who translated Bolaño into English. I'm not going to leave anything to chance. I'm going to film this one Hitchcock-style, the planning's going to be obsessive. When I get to set, I almost won't need to direct.

He turned to leave the basement, clutching the Oscar and my forearm, murmuring:

We have to kick ass, we have to kick ass, we have to kick ass . . .

It's the first time, in these five years of collaboration, that Santiago has been so vulnerable.

I don't know if I can deal with this pressure.

I can't write under pressure.

There are writers who know how to write under pressure, who need it and even seek it out.

Tony Kushner needs pressure: he charges an advance, lets preproduction go forward, has people standing by and ready to carry out whatever he gives them, knowing that he still has nothing to give them, and once the pressure grows, once people from his own team start knocking on his door and begging him for the finished work, only then does he sit down to write, and he vomits up a masterpiece.

In that situation, I would most likely jump off the balcony, if I happened to have a balcony nearby.

I can't stand pressure.

I can't stand what I write when I write under pressure.

I only function when I write under the illusion that no one is expecting me to write anything.

I function when I write convinced that what I'm writing is not important.

No one is expecting it and it's not important.

That's why the screenplay about the boy who throws his family into a well is the best thing I've written: because no one was waiting for it.

The same thing happened to Charlie Kaufman: his best script is *Being John Malkovich*, because he wrote it when no one was expecting him to write anything; he wrote it for himself, to laugh out loud in his house at night, never imagining that one day it would be produced, that it would be nominated for Best Original Screenplay, that it was going to change his life.

Even in this collaboration with Santiago, I write as if no one were expecting me to write anything, although I know that Santiago sleeps up there above my head and waits for new scenes every day.

But Santiago never rushed me.

He never gave me a deadline.

He never gave me the impression that the scene I'm writing has to be the final version.

I learned to work on the scenes knowing that Santiago was

waiting for them but that there was no rush, I didn't have to get it right on the first try.

This arrangement was enough to allow me to write the way I'd always written, the way I work and that works for me, knowing that what I'm writing in the present tense is not the final version of anything, that it can all be thrown in the trash or rewritten, that it's all meaningless until we decide, taking as much time as necessary, to make it meaningful.

But that arrangement is over.

In this third screenplay, the rules are different.

The rules terrify me.

The rules won't let me write the way I've always written.

The rules are forcing me to become Tony Kushner.

A basemented Tony Kushner.

A Tony Kushner who, when he writes under pressure, writes like shit.

I should tell Santiago that I can't write under these new rules, that I don't agree to stay in the basement under these new rules.

Ha.

You're not in the basement because you agreed to be in the basement, you're in the basement because you have no choice, because you're afraid of dying from a bullet to the brain.

No, it's because you'd hate to miss out on the chance to make art alongside the greatest Latin American film director of all time.

No.

Then why *are* you in the basement?

Why *am* I in the basement?

Why don't I fight to get out, even if by fighting I risk losing my life?

You've already lost your life.

You lost your life the moment you surrendered to that first hug from Santiago.

I wonder how much Santiago cares about Norma, how much affection he has for her.

Maybe if I hold Norma hostage and threaten to kill her, maybe . . .

I'm not going to hold Norma hostage and threaten to kill her.

She'd probably end up killing me.

What do you want, then?

I want to finish the screenplay.

I want to change the history of world cinema, even if no one ever knows I was part of the change.

I want to write a screenplay that is really mine, more mine than the screenplay about the boy who throws his family into a well, more mine than anything I've written until now even if at the same time it is not mine at all; a screenplay that belongs entirely to Santiago Salvatierra, because *he* is the genius, *he* is the one who transformed my failed screenplays into movies that changed the history of Latin American cinema, and soon, if I don't let the pressure paralyze me, the history of world cinema.

*   *   *

Page forty-seven.

The second act is made of sand, sand that dribbles from the sides of the screen onto the floor.

The same thing used to happen to me when I first started to write: the sentences fell from the screen.

The floor would be littered with words that refused to form part of my shitty texts, words that I felt on the soles of my feet.

I'd bought myself a cheap PC.

I didn't know what to do with my life.

Studying music had been a mistake, a waste of time, not because of the music (playing an instrument is useful, understanding the Beatles is useful), but because a career as a session musician turned out to be a dead end, or rather a path that led me, in less than two years, off a cliff.

The guitar, the amp, and the music stand holding scores and exercises in auditory perception and musical literacy only reminded me of my mistake.

I sold it all.

All except for the four-piece Technics stereo and the Beatles albums.

I hid the money deep in my sock drawer.

Until one morning my old lady mentioned that she wanted to design a website for her children's party act; she wanted to put up photos and videos and the prices of the different kinds of activities.

I took the money from the depths of my sock drawer and I bought a cheap, disassembled PC.

I was going to build it myself.

Since I knew nothing about computers, I thought that if I bought one disassembled and put it together myself I would learn a lot in a short time.

It took me two weeks to put it together.

I had to assemble it, disassemble it, assemble, disassemble, go to the store to exchange the graphics card, and assemble it again.

I had to install Windows, uninstall it, and install it again.

My old lady hired a private tutor who taught her how to use Outlook, Word, and Excel, and how to design a simple web page.

One night (I couldn't sleep in the heat; it was summer and my old lady hated to sleep with the air conditioner on), I got out of bed and went to the kitchen to drink a glass of water.

The PC was asleep, next to the fridge.

It made me mad how that machine could sleep so peacefully.

I sat down and moved the mouse: the monitor turned on.

My old lady had left Outlook open—her work emails.

I closed it.

She had also left Word open on a page where she'd written:

"We have *mate* how delicious is *mate* how delicious it is."

I saved her . . . poem? on the desktop and opened a blank document.

I sat for a long time staring at that blank page on the PC I'd put together with my own hands and didn't know how to use, or what to use it for, thinking it would be best to just go back to bed, lie down beside my mother, and try to sleep.

But it was impossible to sleep in that heat.

I thought about going out for a walk.

But no, I stayed still before the blank page, listening to the PC emit its robotic hum.

At a certain point, I leaned over the keyboard and typed the words "I write."

I sat for a long time staring at the words "I write" on the screen.

Then I typed the words "I read."

What kind of horseshit was this?

"I write. I read."

"I write I read I write I read."

I went back into the bedroom trying to make as little noise as possible and picked up my book from the floor.

Since there was no room for night tables, we left our things on the floor: a book, a pair of glasses, Kleenex, cell phone, the photo of my father that my old lady kissed every morning and every night.

The used book of the moment: *The Magic Mountain.*

I settled the book in next to the keyboard, opened it on a page in the middle, and typed one of Mann's sentences.

I sat for a long time staring at that sentence.

A sentence that didn't belong to me, but that, separated from the text, alone on that Word document on a cheap computer at the ass end of the world, *seemed* like mine.

I don't know how long I spent staring at that sentence, but suddenly I leaned over the keyboard again and typed another sentence, this time mine, beside Mann's.

I sat for a long time staring at the two sentences.

My old lady got up to go to the bathroom and asked me what I was doing.

Nothing, I told her, I couldn't sleep.

She started to say something, but no, she went into the bathroom, peed, flushed, came out of the bathroom, and went back to bed.

I spent the rest of the night writing.

A story.

A horrible story, begun admirably by Mann and ruined by me.

A fifteen-page story.

Fifteen pages in just a few hours.

I was tired when I finished, and happy, though I didn't understand why I felt happy.

It was a pleasant exhaustion, one I'd never felt before, not even when I managed to finish a guitar exercise without making any mistakes.

It was a mental exhaustion, not remotely physical, though I did also feel it in my body.

I saved the story in a file I called Drafts, and I saved Drafts in My Computer.

I lay down in the bed when my old lady was waking up.

I quickly fell asleep to the sound of her making *mate*.

The next day I read the story once, and without hesitating for a second, I moved it to the Recycling Bin and emptied the Recycling Bin.

I made a cup of Dolca instant coffee with milk, sat down at the PC, opened a Word document, and started to write.

I wanted to find out what it was that had brought on that perfect tiredness in me: if it was simply writing a lot, or the idea that I was writing something good, or if it just had to do with sitting in front of a computer screen for hours on end.

I wrote a twenty-five-page story in one sitting.

I drank three Dolcas with milk.

The exhaustion was the same—perfect, the kind of peace available only to dogs.

Even though this second time I'd written with the certainty that what I was writing was shit, literary garbage.

I stored that second story in the Drafts file in My Computer.

The next morning I read it again, put it in the Recycling Bin, and emptied the Recycling Bin.

That's how I spent the following months: writing a story a day between fifteen and forty pages long, and the next morning I'd read the story and throw it in the Recycling Bin and empty the Recycling Bin.

I'd never felt so good.

It was as if a psychiatrist had given me a prescription for a benzodiazepine and told me to take it every day, no side effects, no fear of getting hooked.

But I did get hooked.

Hooked on writing those pages every day.

Hooked on writing a shitty story a day.

If I didn't write my shitty story, I felt like the day had been wasted.

I typed on that PC like a crazed monkey.

I started to notice the noise my old lady made: everything my mother did in the apartment while I was writing (things she'd done for years and that had never bothered me before) started to echo as if amplified by a megaphone.

I bought a notebook and went to a bar to write.

I practically stopped reading during that time.

I just wrote, hours and hours, the world around me a blur, and then I tore up the pages into little pieces and threw them into the trash.

I didn't save anything I wrote that year.

That's not true.

I saved a detective novel that I wrote in one go.

If I remember correctly, I started it at two in the afternoon in the bar on the corner and finished it at four in the morning on the PC, overdosing on instant coffee and milk while my old lady snored away in the bedroom.

A detective novel called *Absolutely Still* that I wrote with a lot of excitement even if later I realized it didn't work, at least not entirely (I was too lazy to fix it).

A detective novel that I wrote without knowing where it was going, without knowing what the answer to the mystery was.

I surprised myself when I caught a glimpse of the answer, on page sixty-something.

It was a detective novel that I was reading at the same time I was writing it, and that's likely why it didn't work.

It's best to plan ahead before writing a detective novel, structure it the same way we structure screenplays, toil over the structure before you ever sit down to write the first word.

I always liked reading detective novels, though most of them are idiotic and predictable.

There's something soothing about that kind of novel.

Every four books I traded in at used bookstores, I chose a detective novel; three books of "serious literature" and one detective novel.

I really enjoyed reading those detective novels when they weren't idiotic and predictable, much more than I enjoyed books of "serious literature."

Except when I read Beckett's trilogy.

Sorry: Beckett's "three novels."

Beckett didn't like his "three novels" to be called a "trilogy."

Molloy, *Malone Dies*, and *The Unnamable*.

There is something detective-esque in those books of supposed "serious literature"—especially in *Molloy*, although also toward the end of *Malone Dies*.

At Librería Norte I bought a box set put out by Alianza Editorial, printed on cheap paper, badly bound, with barely legible print.

I read and reread those books over the course of a year, without stopping, without alternating them with other books, until I felt repelled by those same three novels; I started to get angry at them (not so much at *Malone Dies*, but at the other two; I got sick of *Malone Dies*, too, but I didn't get angry at it), and then I took Beckett's three novels to the used bookstore and traded them in for *Operation Shylock* by Philip Roth.

* * *

Santiago bites his nails.

These past few days, while we work, he's been biting his nails nonstop.

Every once in a while he looks at them, examines them, lets out a snort, and goes on biting them.

Yesterday I wrote an important scene.

I felt good after writing it, calm.

Santiago came down this morning and looked at me in that way he looks at me when he reads something I wrote and thinks it's good: an expression that's hard to interpret, as if he felt hatred and pride at the same time, as if it bothered him enormously that I'd written a scene that works, and at the same time he wanted to hug me and call me "son."

The scene I wrote yesterday knocked down a wall: for the first time in weeks the second act has shape, it seems to be within the realm of possibility.

Santiago is in a good mood; he bites his nails nonstop and smiles at anything.

He was never one to laugh at my jokes, but now he laughs at all my jokes.

His jokes are always bad, and he always laughs at them, and he looks at me expecting me to laugh, too, convinced that his jokes are all great and brilliant and fresh.

His jokes are all bad and stupid and passé.

But I laugh.

Of course I laugh.

Another price that I pay: jaw pain.

Santiago is so convinced of his genius that he can't conceive of the possibility that anyone could laugh insincerely at his jokes; when it comes to his jokes, forced laughter does not exist.

We're having a tough time finding humor in the script.

Light moments.

Santiago forces light moments to the utmost, convinced they can be dredged up by sheer will.

But the only light moments that work are the ones that appear naturally, the ones that aren't strong-armed into the scene, but revealed unexpectedly.

Sometimes when I'm writing a dramatic, melancholy scene, my mind offers up a spark of light, and I can't let it pass, I have to work it into the scene immediately.

That's how any worthwhile light moment appears.

But in this third screenplay the sparks are in short supply, and Santiago is starting to force them: he tries to convince me he's felt one when in reality he hasn't felt a thing, he's just making it up.

If they don't come, they don't come.

The script is a little what we want it to be, a little what it wants to be.

It . . . Is a screenplay a he? Or a she?

The first screenplay I wrote for Santiago was a he, the second was a she.

This one, maybe, is a hermaphrodite script.

Or an asexual screenplay.

Okay, then, the asexual screenplay lacks humor.

Like Santiago, who also lacks humor.

The humor depends on me, and this time it isn't coming.

So far, this screenplay holds only darkness, and a screenplay of only darkness will never be the year's Best Picture.

A movie that is only darkness can win the Oscar for Best Foreign Film, but not for Best Picture.

The days fly by.

I never imagined days in the basement could fly by.

Norma brought down a Red Bull with lunch.

I asked her what the deal was with the Red Bull, I shouted that I didn't ask for it, but as always, she said nothing.

She doesn't have to tell me what the deal is with the Red Bull: Santiago is desperate.

Our third film is going to cost a fortune: no less than seventy million dollars.

Santiago never filmed with more than fifteen million, which is a ton of money for a movie in Spanish.

But this third film must have a budget of no less than seventy million, and that's if everything goes well, if it all goes off without a hitch, and in Santiago's productions there are always hitches.

His demands grow in a way that's inversely proportional to the preestablished budget.

I have to admit the Red Bull works; I asked Norma to bring another one with dinner.

I remember one year ago, when I sat down at the computer loaded up on caffeine, ready to write a story I was obsessed with.

A story that, like everything I wrote during that time, I wrote in one sitting.

A story about a pedophile priest who was sentenced to thirty years in jail, and after a decade of silence and confinement he agrees to let a journalist interview him and explains (to the journalist) that he'd never wanted to abuse those boys, that he was no degenerate, all he'd been trying to do was make love with Baby Jesus.

I remember my old lady's face when she read the story.

I don't know why I gave her that story to read; I never showed her anything I wrote.

I guess there was something about that story that placed it above the others.

Was I proud of having written the story about the pedophile priest?

A horrible, shocking story, but superior to everything I had written before.

Yes, it was the first time I felt proud of something I'd written.

But my old lady's face forced me to throw the story into the Recycling Bin and empty the Recycling Bin.

I didn't want to be responsible for a story that brought that expression to my mother's face.

I gave her the detective novel, *Absolutely Still*; I printed it out for her at an internet café on A4 paper and in Times New Roman, 14-point, single-spaced.

It took her a week to read it.

She told me she liked it a lot, that she'd been surprised by the ending, that she was impressed I had been able to write something like that.

First time my old lady ever said she was impressed by something I had done.

She was never impressed by my musical achievements.

She'd looked at me with pity, a smile full of pity, a smile that told me: "I'm going to support you in whatever you want to do," and at the same time: "What a sad future I see for you in music."

It's depressing to write about my old lady.

I imagine what she must have felt when I disappeared.

Even though I can't imagine it, I imagine it, and it disturbs me to imagine it.

Sometimes I think my old lady would have agreed to live with me here in the basement.

She would have helped me help the all-time greatest Latin American film director become the world's all-time greatest film director.

My old lady was the one who convinced me to stop throwing what I wrote into the Recycling Bin.

Take as long as you want, she told me, but write something worthwhile. *Something worthwhile to you.* Something you want to show people. I'll fix you all the Dolcas with milk you need. Don't rush. If it takes you a year, take a year. If it takes two, take two.

It took three.

Three years during which I wrote five stories, none of them longer than ten pages.

That is, I wrote many more, but those five stories were the only ones I thought were worth anything.

Clearly I couldn't put together a book from five stories no longer than ten pages each.

My old lady told me to add the detective novel, but no, *Absolutely Still* belonged to another era, it had been written during my training years.

It doesn't have anything to do with these five new stories, I told her.

My old lady seemed to understand, but she started to look at me again with her pitying smile.

Lisandro told me that one of his cousins had a little house on Chascomús Lake.

If you want, he told me, I can ask if you can borrow it. You can go for a few days. You lock yourself in the house and write until you finish at least ten more stories. Then I'll help you send the book to publishers.

I never really liked to travel, especially alone, but Chascomús is only an hour and a half from the Capital, and it didn't hurt to try.

My old lady offered to pay the carfare.

I got to Lisandro's cousin's house on a Tuesday morning.

It was raining.

The house smelled damp and moldy.

Every nook and cranny held a spiderweb.

I spent the first few hours cleaning, getting rid of all the bugs I found, making sure the screens fit snugly in the doors and windows.

I stocked the fridge with cartons of SanCor whole milk, Cepita orange juice, and packets of Vieníssima hot dogs.

In the pantry I stowed hot dog buns, mayonnaise, ketchup, mustard, a large jar of Dolca instant coffee, Vainillas Capri cookies, and 9 de Oro biscuits.

The first two days I didn't leave the house.

I sat in the kitchen and tried to write in a notebook: a while in the morning, a while in the afternoon, and a while at night.

Then I would try to sleep, or read, or masturbate.

I'd brought two novels by Cormac McCarthy (*Suttree* and *Blood Meridian*), Flannery O'Connor's *Complete Works*, and an ancient *Hustler* that I bought at one of those used book and magazine shops on Corrientes Avenue.

Everything I wrote those first two days, I crossed out.

The morning of the third day I picked up speed with a story about a writer who shuts himself away in a house full of bugs on Chascomús Lake to write, and he eats nothing but hot dogs and vanilla wafers and he overdoses on Dolca instant coffee with milk, but he can't manage to write what he wants to write, and then he stands at the kitchen window and writes descriptions in a notebook of the different shades of the sky, the shapes of the clouds, etc.

The afternoon of the fifth day I left the house and walked to the lake.

I sat on a rock and looked at the water.

There was nothing special about that accumulation of water.

It was just a lake, one that, like any tourist destination, leaves plenty to be desired.

A lake that doesn't reveal what is special about nature, but rather what is mundane about it, what is taken for granted, what no one would mourn if it suddenly ceased to exist.

I opened *Blood Meridian* and read a few pages.

Nothing made sense; that agglomeration of incredibly well-written violence was entirely worthless.

I thought, sitting on the rock, looking at the brownish water, that if Cormac McCarthy disappeared (that is, if he'd never existed), the world would be exactly the same; that if Faulkner were snatched from history, the world would be exactly the same; that if Shakespeare were snatched from history . . .

A bird landed beside me.

I don't know what kind of bird it was. It looked like a pigeon, but not quite.

It perched for a while not doing anything, moving in that manic way birds move, and then it looked at me, its bird eyes stared at me, it cawed, it kept looking at me, and then it flapped its wings and flew off.

I closed the Cormac McCarthy book.

The sun went down in front of me, disappearing behind the trees.

I was surprised by how fast the sun went down; in just a few minutes it was hidden, the sky was no longer blue and the clouds were dyed a dark pink that reminded me of the cotton candy my old man used to buy me when we went to the Rodas circus.

I thought about how that sky and those clouds were impossible to write, how no one, no matter how much talent or genius he has, could write that sky and those clouds.

I realized why I had always detested naturalist literature.

I had read the great books of world literature skipping entire paragraphs of description.

No one—past, present, or future—will ever be able to put into words that sky and those clouds suspended before me over that depressing lake.

I went back to the house, called my mother, and told her I was coming home.

She asked me how it had gone.

I didn't answer.

I stashed the few clothes I had brought in my bag, left the house, locked the door, walked along the lake until I came across a woman drinking *mate* in the grass, and I asked her where I could catch a bus to the Capital.

*   *   *

More or less a year later, I was finishing my first screenplay.

In some three hundred days I had said goodbye to literature and hello to film, an art that I hardly knew beyond going to the movies about ten times a year, starting when my parents had taken me to see *E.T.* at the Pinamar theater (my first movie) and I cried like a dumbass through the whole third act.

Santiago says that film is the best of the art forms because it incorporates all the others: film uses literature, painting, theater, music, photography, sculpture. It uses the widest array of the sciences.

In my opinion (I've never told Santiago this), film uses all the other arts and the widest array of the sciences, but it doesn't go deep into any of them; it uses a few drops from all the arts, but it doesn't squeeze all the juice out of any of them.

You can make film knowing a little about painting, or a little about theater, or a little about literature.

It is an art that's tailor-made for these times, when most artists (including Santiago, including me) don't know much about anything, they don't squeeze the juice out of any one discipline.

Film is an industrial art, and for that reason it is deeply imperfect.

The more people who participate, the more imperfect the result.

A sum of imperfections.

One person's genius is diluted in the mediocrity of the rest.

I didn't say goodbye to literature and hello to film because I thought that the art of film was superior to the art of literature.

No, the art of film is clearly inferior to the art of literature.

No art (except music) reaches such a level of profundity, of intimacy between artist and audience, as literature does.

None of the other narrative arts have been able to surpass literature yet; not cinema, not theater, not television.

But it requires an extreme level of commitment to write literature.

The writer must live to write his books.

Everything else in his life is an obstacle: family, friends—entities that only hinder him, keep him from spending more hours writing.

I realized that I was incapable of such commitment, and that, had I been capable, the result wouldn't have been worth it.

The commitment-to-result ratio would have left me in the red.

A screenplay, on the other hand, calls for a different kind of commitment.

The screenplay is an aliterary text.

It doesn't have style.

That is, it doesn't matter if the screenwriter imprints his style on the page.

There are many screenwriters with many different styles, but ultimately none of those styles matter, they end up tucked away in the drawers full of produced or unproduced screenplays.

I like to sit down to write without having to worry about style.

I don't have to be Joyce, or Hemingway, or Carver.

I only have to write good scenes: clear directions, precise dialogues.

It's more about what I avoid than what I don't.

That first screenplay that I finished a year after returning from the house on Chascomús wasn't worthwhile, it was essentially bad, but I wasn't ashamed of it the way I was ashamed of the stories.

I showed it to Lisandro.

He congratulated me, then told me to make it disappear.

But I didn't throw it in the Recycling Bin, I saved it in a folder in My Computer called Screenplays.

Lisandro had started to work as a production assistant at his uncle's advertising production company.

I asked him to get me screenplays; it didn't matter which ones, I just wanted to read screenplays, a lot of screenplays, only screenplays.

He got me a book with four screenplays by William Goldman, translated to Spanish: *Butch Cassidy and the Sundance Kid*, *Marathon Man*, *All the President's Men*, and *The Princess Bride*.

I became a William Goldman addict.

I read and reread those screenplays, studied them, retyped them word for word on the PC using a pirated version of Final Draft.

Writing screenplays, though I still didn't know how to do it well, agreed with me.

The kind of sentence that emerged naturally from me when I wrote stories worked better in screenplays.

I spent two years writing screenplays for short and feature-length films.

I finished them, reread them, corrected them, reread them, corrected, reread, and saved them in the Screenplays file in My Computer.

I read piles of books about screenwriting.

I read and reread Aristotle's *Poetics*, because one of those books said that one had to read and reread Aristotle's *Poetics*.

I memorized the essential parts of the *Poetics*, and I put them into practice: I wrote more than twenty screenplays following Aristotle closely.

I bought a DVD player and rented all the movies and TV series that had commentary tracks by screenwriters.

I filled notebooks with the comments that most caught my attention.

I sent some of those short and feature-length screenplays to contests, but I never won; I only got one honorary mention in a contest for shorts, and they gave me the book *Cassavetes on Cassavetes*.

I read and reread *Cassavetes on Cassavetes*.

I read and reread *Lynch on Lynch*, Tarkovsky's *Sculpting in Time*,

Conversations with Woody Allen, and Goldman's *Adventures in the Screen Trade*.

I spent entire weeks locked in the apartment, watching many of the most important movies of film history that I hadn't seen yet, and others that I had seen but didn't remember well, overdosing on instant coffee and milk, sometimes with my mother drinking *mate* beside me.

I kept writing screenplays, examining them up close, trying to see why they didn't work, how to improve them, how to get the most out of each of the acts, each of the plot points, to understand what the action and conflict was in each screenplay, each scene, what each scene's reversal was, each act's, what each screenplay's subject was, each character's motivation, what obstacle would work best placed in front of or inside each of the characters.

I gave those screenplays to my old lady, to Lisandro, to my girlfriend of the moment if I had one, though I didn't have many girlfriends.

I improved in leaps and bounds as a screenwriter, and they as readers of my screenplays.

My old lady never reproached me for not working (although what I did while shut away in the apartment was, in a way, working).

She never reproached me for not bringing in money; not even when I turned thirty, and then thirty-five.

We weren't ones to spend very much.

We almost never treated ourselves.

We almost never ate out.

We wore the same clothes for years.

The money my old lady earned with her children's party act was enough to cover our medical insurance, food, bills, and a few extra expenses.

There were even months when we had money left over that my old lady stored in a red Lumilagro thermos that she hid in the pantry behind the packages of La Merced *yerba mate*.

I hope that in these past five years she's saved enough to ensure some level of comfort in her old age.

* * *

Santiago slammed the door on his way out.

We worked the usual hours, and when he was getting ready to leave, when he picked up his chair and headed for the door, I asked him to wait a second.

I told him that I don't plan to keep writing if he doesn't get a check to my mother for one hundred thousand dollars.

He looked at me the way he looks at me when I say something he doesn't entirely understand, or that he does understand but needs a few seconds to digest.

How do you expect me to justify a check for a hundred thousand dollars for a woman I don't know? he asked me.

Doesn't matter, I said. Not my problem. I'm sure you made a lot of money with the movies I wrote for you, and I'm also sure that you're going to make even more money with this one I'm writing now. The least you can do is—

You're writing a movie for me? You wrote movies for me? Where did you get that idea? Where is your name on these movies you supposedly wrote for me?

He grabbed the chair by its backrest and threw it against the wall.

You are helping me, Pablo, he said. That's all you do. You help me. You have the privilege of helping me, and that way you get to be part of a historic event. No one does anything for me in my movies. I do it all. I even act in them. I light them, I edit them, I compose their music, and I design the costumes and the sound. Other people help me. They're my assistants. Because you can't make a movie completely alone. Much less a movie that's going to change the history of world cinema.

I asked him why he didn't write the next scene, then.

Take all the time you want, I told him. Write it, bring it down, and we'll read it.

He looked at me the way he looks at me when he wishes with all his heart that I were a dead body, a body in an advanced stage of decomposition.

I'm not going to write anything, he said. That's why you're here. I give you the scenes, you write them. The scenes are mine, the writing yours. It's all you have, the writing, the act of writing. The scenes are mine, the characters are mine.

I'm only asking you to take care of my mother in her old age, I told him. It's not so much to ask. A hundred thousand dollars. The same amount you spend on sandwiches for the film crew to snack on between scenes. A hundred thousand dollars, Santiago. The way my old lady lives, that money will last her twenty years. If you don't want to give her a check in your name, ask your accountant to take the money out in cash and Norma can take it to her.

And what is your mother going to think? Will she accept a hundred thousand dollars as a gift from a woman she doesn't know?

We can invent an excuse.

Like what? What excuse, Pablo?

I don't know. Let me think. I'll come up with something.

No, I don't want you spending your time thinking up excuses to get your mother to accept money that isn't hers. I want you to write the scenes we need. We're only now getting into the second half of the second act. There's a lot left to write, and we don't have much time. Write, Pablo. Write my scenes. Stop staring at me like a moron and get writing.

Santiago's slammed doors are ever more exaggerated, melo-dramatic; the closer we get to finishing the screenplay, the more exaggerated and melodramatic his slammed doors.

I'm writing this sitting on the floor with my back against the door, and I can still feel the vibrations.

*   *   *

I don't know why it didn't occur to me sooner to ask Santiago to take care of my old lady, to set her up for the little life she has left.

I'm troubled and terrified by the question of why I didn't feel the need sooner to ask Santiago to take care of my old lady.

I'm troubled and terrified by the ease with which I accepted my life in the basement, my reality as a basemented writer.

Why did it never occur to me to ask Santiago to pay me?

Because I've been abducted, and no one pays an abductee?

But abductees don't usually work for their abductors.

Or do they?

Am I like those kidnapped Chinese people who make knockoff handbags?

No, those Chinese people aren't kidnapped, per se; they wanted to escape their country, they paid to get out, and they make knock-off handbags because they still owe money, they have to save an exorbitant amount of money, but once they do that they can leave and do what they want with their lives.

I guess.

The truth is I don't know anything about those Chinese people who make knockoff handbags.

I never made money.

Maybe that's why I can't imagine anyone having to pay me to write screenplays.

I'm about to turn forty-six years old, and I never earned a paycheck.

I never paid taxes.

I was never even self-employed.

I never had a credit card.

I lived for twenty-four years off my parents, sixteen off my mother, and I've lived five off of Santiago.

I only sold one screenplay, in Buenos Aires, but they didn't pay me a cent.

The director and producers told me that no one was going to get paid up front, not even the actors, because they had barely enough money to produce the movie, but that when it was released everyone would receive part of the earnings.

They put a contract in front of me that said my payment would be zero pesos, but that the future earnings would be divided into one hundred points, of which three points would be mine, and according to them, this was an excellent arrangement for me.

How could I be so naive as to believe that movie was ever going to make money, that it would turn a profit?

Maybe I wasn't so naive as to think the movie was going to make money, maybe I just didn't give a fuck.

I never gave a fuck about money.

I never imagined that anything I wrote could make money.

The profit of writing was in the very act of writing.

That's why I'm sitting here at this hour of the early morning, with the glass brick rectangle completely black, to write in this encrypted file.

Writing is the only thing that matters about writing; it's the only thing that *should* matter.

Maybe I don't give a fuck about money because I never needed it; there was always enough at home to cover the basic necessities;

I always relied on my folks, like I rely on Santiago now.

Did the basement set me up for life?

Did my abduction set me up for life?

I am, clearly, a complacent person.

My old man was a complacent guy; he lived in the comfort of his routine, and he hated everything that forced him to break it.

He hated vacations.

Whenever my old lady convinced him to take a family holiday, spend a few days in Pinamar or Mar del Plata, my old man sank into an acutely terrible mood that lasted for weeks.

Usually, he wouldn't emerge from that acutely terrible mood until the moment we settled into the house in Pinamar or Mar del Plata and he unpacked all his things and managed to glimpse what his routine would be like for the rest of the vacation.

Before the trip, he could spend an entire day complaining about the noise the shower door made when you slid it to get in or out of the shower.

A freezer that didn't close well could drive him to punch a wall and injure his hand.

He only accepted trips calmly when they were for work, and that was because they were part of his routine, and also they were completely taken care of: from the car that would pick him up at home to the car that was waiting for him at the airport to take him to the hotel, from priority check-in to priority boarding to the executive lounge and the executive-class seat and the papers that avoided any trouble at immigration.

My old man didn't do anything on those trips other than go to the duty-free shops and write down every detail, both spatial and human, in his little notebook with the cream-colored cover.

He didn't visit the cities, just settled into a hotel near the airport and spent his free time in his room watching the news.

My old man loved news shows.

Once, I asked him why he had such love for the news, and he said he liked to see what was happening in the world.

I like to know the world is there, he told me, that it exists and it's immense and quite often horrendous. The news shows let me see what's happening in the world without my having to participate in the world.

I told him that in my opinion the news shows were a distorted window.

He took a sip of his finger of Johnnie Walker Black Label (he was capable of making that finger of Johnnie Walker last an hour), and he told me we were all distorted windows.

All of us, Pablo. There is no person in the world who is not a distorted window.

My old man had enormous potential; if he had wanted to, he could have changed the world in the discipline of his choosing, but instead he repressed that enormous potential in exchange for a simple, comfortable life.

My old man could have been Santiago Salvatierra, maybe even greater than Santiago Salvatierra, but he chose to live as an employee of the millionaire owner of twenty-five percent of the world's duty-free shops.

Santiago has never been anyone's employee, not even of the financiers who financed his films, or of the brands or producers who hired him to film commercials.

He's never filmed anything without making sure he had the final cut.

I respect him for that.

He hasn't accepted a single one of the projects the Hollywood studios offered him.

In these last few years Santiago could have directed a new

Indiana Jones or Star Wars movie, or any of the superhero movies that broke box office records, but no, he only films what he wants to film, only stories that belong to him.

He meets with the financiers and executive producers of his movies, and he listens to their comments, and he tries to seem open, respectful, but in the end, he always does what he wants.

That's why the budgets of his films tend to go to shit.

That's why several of the actors he's worked with don't want to lay eyes on him ever again—because sometimes, to get the result he wanted, he had to torture them.

Months and months of torture.

Actors who do what they want and get what they want ninety-five percent of all the hours of their lives were subjected to months and months of torture.

That's why Ricardo Darín was ready to beat the shit out of him at the after-party of the premiere for the only movie they made together.

That's why Antonio Banderas, when he finished the final scene—after the entire crew applauded the end of filming for a full minute—took off his character's clothes and threw them to the ground, in front of everyone, and locked himself in his trailer and didn't come out again.

Santiago knows there are a lot of people who don't want to ever lay eyes on him again, but he doesn't care.

I respect him for that, too.

Movies are more important than the people who make them, Pablo, he once told me. *Much* more important. Movies are all that matter. The movies are going to survive us. They're going to be *us* when we aren't here anymore. They're going to be *me*. A *me* made of the most perfect images.

I reread the first act and what I have of the second.

I'm burning through the days left to finish the screenplay even before I live them.

It's best not to think.

Not to organize.

Not to set a number of pages per day, or a number of scenes per week.

The best thing is to write, to go on writing, and let God take it from there.

*   *   *

Today, before Santiago came down with his chair, the cup of coffee, the little dish of fruit, and the printed scenes with his notes, I erased the chalkboard; I spat onto a paper napkin and erased the Aristotelian diagramming of the second act, the list of important plot points for each character, and the list of themes to develop.

Santiago didn't like finding the chalkboard empty.

My saliva smells like rotten fish.

He stood for a long time looking at the empty chalkboard, and then he turned, handed me the little dish of fruit, and told me that the scenes I wrote yesterday were the best I've written in ages.

I have almost no notes, he said. Just a couple little things. If we keep it up at this rate, we'll finish on time. I talked to Meryl Streep yesterday. She's in. She was so in love with her character that she said she's in without even reading the script. Though she's dying to read it. The best actress in the history of film is going to read our script, Pablo. She's going to memorize it. She's going to chew it all up and swallow it, until it becomes hers. Our words are going to be Meryl Streep's words.

More pressure.

Now when the character opens her mouth, when I write the

words that come out of the character's mouth, I think about Meryl Streep's mouth.

It's the first time Santiago has talked to me about casting.

He never invites me to participate in other areas.

He never shows me photos of locations, or videos of casting sessions.

He only lets me suggest music—albums that could inspire a future soundtrack, albums that he generally ends up not liking.

Santiago makes a great effort to reject what other people (friends, or members of his film crew, or producers, or actors) propose to him.

He doesn't like knowing that something in his films wasn't his idea and didn't come from him.

What he does (at least what he's always done with me) is reject what I propose, study it and reject it (he said no to each and every one of the albums I asked him to download and that he bought on iTunes), and then, some weeks later, he transforms that suggestion of mine into his, he appropriates it, as if I were such an imbecile as to not realize, to not remember that I was the one who suggested such and such an album.

He has so much nerve that he's capable of walking out of the basement totally convinced that I didn't even notice, that there's no chance I remember it was me who proposed such and such an album.

Really, I don't know if Santiago does the same thing with his friends, or the members of his film crews, or his producers, or actors; it wouldn't surprise me if he did, if he were also capable of turning those people's suggestions into his own.

I envy Santiago's nerve.

How much easier my life would have been if I'd had just a few ounces of his nerve.

Where would I be now if I'd been born with half a pound of Santiago's nerve?

Married?

With children?

Living in a house in La Lucila with a roomy studio where I could shut myself in and write, and a library full of books?

Would I still have thrown those stories I wrote in one sitting into the PC's Recycling Bin and then emptied the Recycling Bin?

Or would I have saved them, polished and rewritten them a little, and then sent them to publishers?

Would one of those publishers have accepted my stories?

Would they have accepted my failed detective novel?

Absolutely Still: over a million copies sold, translated into thirty languages, the rights sold to Hollywood.

Santiago wouldn't have been able to kidnap me, because everyone would have wondered where the successful Argentine novelist had gotten to.

Maybe, if this third screenplay lets Santiago film the movie he dreams of filming, the one that will change the history of world cinema, maybe then he'll let me go.

It doesn't sound all that far-fetched.

Once you win it all, there's nothing left.

I don't think he'd lose much if he let me go, or that I could put him in danger.

Who's going to believe a crazy, bearded guy pushing fifty who says that the world's greatest director locked him in a basement and forced him to write screenplays?

Santiago has nothing to lose.

That's what I thought today, all day long.

Now, sitting on the mattress with the laptop on my lap, I'm not so sure.

Santiago isn't one to leave loose ends—not in art, and not in life.

A perfect blend of Fellini and Hitchcock: half great poet, half compulsive workaholic.

I don't know what Santiago is going to do with me if this third screenplay lets him film the movie he dreams of filming.

I do know what he's going to do if the movie doesn't change the history of world cinema: he's going to ask me to write another one.

He's going to spend hours talking to me about the importance of art, the kind of art that will be *us* once we are no more.

He's going to promise me that this time he has the right story, the best story for the best movie ever filmed, and I'm going to say yes.

And I'm going to listen to his story, and I'm going to work on it with him, structure it, diagram it, and then I'll write it for him.

That's why I have to make sure that this third screenplay is the one that changes the history of world cinema.

This third screenplay has to let Santiago film the movie that he dreams of filming, it has to make him into the world's greatest director; no matter what, it has to win him the Oscar for Best Picture.

No, the Palme d'Or and the Oscar for Best Picture, both in the same year, for the first time in history.

I don't sleep.

Two, two and a half hours at most.

I think tonight I'm going to stop trying.

If my mind doesn't want to sleep, then I'm going to put it to work.

Fuck it.

Two nights ago I took Borges's *Complete Works* from the medicine cabinet and read a couple of stories in the hopes they would make me sleepy.

No dice.

I tried a couple of essays, but the essays tend to be better written than the stories and I got hooked, until a sentence in the second paragraph of "Valéry as Symbol" drove me to the laptop and this encrypted file.

Santiago went to Los Angeles, and he'll be back in a week.

He asked me to try to finish at least the third quarter of the second act.

Sometimes directors talk about screenplays as if they were Excel spreadsheets.

People who don't know how to write are never going to understand what it is to write.

On several occasions I tried to explain what writing is to my old lady and Lisandro, and although they said yes, they understood, I could tell they hadn't understood a thing.

I don't want to sound pedantic, but it's the truth: people who don't write will never have even the remotest idea of what it is to write.

I don't give a fuck about sounding pedantic.

Not even people who write because they think writing can do something for them, the ones who sign up for literary workshops, who read a book they like and think they can write something just as good, who study Literature and major in Screenwriting, who write a page a month and carry a notebook with them everywhere and underline books and fill their margins with bullshit—not even those people have the slightest fucking idea what it means to write.

Santiago is going to die as one of the most successful screenwriters in the history of cinema, all without having the slightest fucking idea of what it means to write.

My hands are shaking.

Must be lack of sleep.

Must be the awareness that instead of writing this shit I should be writing scenes.

What if I fail?

What if instead of writing the screenplay that lets Santiago make the movie he dreams of, the one that's going to change the course of world cinema history, I write a shitty screenplay?

What if I just start to type the first thing that comes into my head?

Writers who think the first thing that comes into their heads is good don't have the slightest fucking idea what writing is.

Writing well (that is, really writing) is an excavation job, an archaeological dig into oneself, chipping away at the layers of mediocrity until you find what's really worthwhile.

Writers who believe they're Mozart are never going to write anything worthwhile (that is, unless they're Mozart).

What if I give my fingers over to the crust of mediocrity that covers me entirely?

Maybe Santiago will be disappointed in me and he'll let me go.

No, more likely he'll blow my head off with one shot.

For being mediocre.

To avoid any problems in the future, yes, but above all for being mediocre: to erase my mediocrity from the world.

It's also likely he would realize I was doing it on purpose.

He would *most likely* realize I was doing it on purpose.

It's also likely that in my attempt to write a bad screenplay, I'd end up writing the most successful screenplay I'd ever written.

The worst in quality, but the most successful.

Mediocrity generates empathy.

But Santiago would never agree to direct that screenplay.

Maybe he would agree to executive produce it—he executive produces a ton of movies that at their best are merely passable; it's as if he agrees to sponsor only directors he knows are worse than him, *much* worse, as if he offers his name as charity.

*   *   *

When Santiago is away, Norma comes down with the revolver tucked into her apron pocket.

Only once did she point it at me, right at my face.

It was one night while Santiago was filming our second movie (or promoting it), when I refused to eat the dinner she'd served me with her usual blank expression.

I told her I was not about to eat brains.

I hate *sesos*, I told her. I'm not a zombie, Norma. I don't eat brains, whether they come from a cow or some guy from Neuquén.

She looked at me.

I thought she was going to say something, but no, she pulled the revolver out of her apron pocket and aimed it right at my face.

With her foot, she pushed the tray with the plate of *sesos* and pureed squash toward me.

I told her Santiago didn't force me to eat if I didn't want to eat.

I hate *sesos*, Norma, I repeated. Just looking at them makes me want to throw up.

She picked the tray up with one hand, never lowering the gun, and left the basement.

That night she didn't come to air the place out.

The next morning she brought breakfast at a random time.

For several days she changed up my schedule, ruined my routine.

She did a half-assed job of cleaning the basement, too; she forgot to change my towels, and to replace the toilet paper.

Sometimes she came down with a portable radio and listened to Mexican *rancheras*.

If I was listening to the Beatles, she'd turn up the radio as loud as it would go, and I'd be forced to turn off my music.

The months Santiago spends producing or filming or promoting movies last for years in the basement.

I usually don't do anything during those months.

I eat, and sleep, and read one of the books Santiago has upstairs in his library and that Norma begrudgingly brings down with the food when I ask, and I listen to the Beatles, and I masturbate, and this time, when Santiago leaves to preproduce and shoot and promote this third movie, I'll be able to play songs on the ukelele, too—assuming Santaolalla doesn't ask Santiago to return it to him—including Mexican *rancheras* for Norma when she cleans.

I no longer suffer attacks of desperation or claustrophobia.

I did suffer attacks of desperation and claustrophobia the first few months I was left with nothing to do, when Santiago went off to preproduce and shoot and promote our first movie.

I couldn't stop thinking about my old lady.

Alone, suffering from my disappearance.

I always pictured her the same way: sitting at the kitchen table with her *mate*, staring out at the sunrise.

A sunrise that is no longer a sunrise, because of me, because of Santiago.

A ruined sunrise.

A sunrise that I sometimes see framed in the rectangle of glass bricks, though I'm aware it's not really the sunrise.

A sunrise projected by the noon sun.

A sunrise I avoided during those first idle months, alone in the basement, with nothing to do but pass the time.

I started reading biographies.

I don't know why.

I asked Norma to bring down every biography in Santiago's library.

I read the life stories of Schopenhauer, Dostoyevsky, Ayrton

Senna, Chekhov, Miles Davis, Marco Polo, Teddy Roosevelt, Malcolm Lowry.

I reread Malcolm Lowry's biography.

Three times I read Malcolm Lowry's biography.

I wrote something based on his adolescence, a long story, or maybe a short novel, another of those bursts of writing without thinking about what I was writing, without structuring, just putting one sentence after another, one word after another, one letter after another.

Is there any other way to write?

Is it worth it to write any other way?

I called the long story or short novel *Jupiter Doesn't Exist* and I hid it in the Utilities folder, in Applications.

It took me a month to write that long story or short novel.

A month of daily struggle against the attacks of desperation and claustrophobia.

A month in which I was on the verge, every single day, usually at night, of shouting to Norma: "Please, take me to a hospital!"

The only thing that relieved my tachycardia was writing that long story or short novel.

Jupiter Doesn't Exist cured me.

Malcolm Lowry cured me.

Writing without knowing where you're going is more effective than going to the psychiatrist.

But you can't write screenplays without knowing where you're going.

You can't write the final draft of a screenplay without knowing where you're going.

You can write the first draft of a screenplay without knowing where you're going, but most likely nothing will be left of that first draft in the final one, or almost nothing.

If you're willing to judge your monster coldly, and to rewrite it, and to throw out everything that needs to be thrown out, even if they're scenes that work individually, then you can write a first draft without knowing where you're going.

If you reach the end of a screenplay feeling that writing it was easy, that there's no great secret to screenwriting, then that draft isn't worth shit.

You have to suffer.

You have to beat your head against the wall.

You have to feel like it's all for nothing.

You have to look at yourself in the mirror and realize your face is idiotic, because we all have idiotic faces—even worse, idiotic *eyes*.

You have to laugh like crazy at least once a week.

You have to cry.

You have to read what you wrote and cry, not because the scenes are sad but because they are pathetic.

You have to spend hours and hours imagining other possible professions.

You have to spend hours and hours thinking up valid excuses, even if they're lies, to justify the failure.

You have to think about suicide.

You have to think seriously about suicide.

You have to roar with laughter about your suicidal thoughts.

You have to force yourself to type, even though you don't feel like typing.

You have to read what you wrote a thousand times, two thousand times, and when you feel like what you're reading is good, you have to pound one of your fingers with a hammer.

You have to accept that you're a shitty writer trying to write something fantastic, something that is far better than you are.

You have to understand that ninety-nine point nine percent of what you are is shit.

You have to search for that zero point one percent of yourself that is worthwhile.

True, you can do everything I've just enumerated (though I didn't technically enumerate) in pajamas at whatever hour you please.

Writing is a difficult but eminently comfortable job.

Writers who say that writing is mostly torture are lying; they say it to scare off the rest of the mortals who hang around wondering whether or not they should dedicate themselves to writing, to keep the competition from growing.

Writing is a comfortable job.

Much more comfortable than any office job.

Much, much more comfortable than any job you'd do in the street, or out in the country, or even in some mode of transportation.

To be a good writer, first of all, you have to be a good slacker.

Slacker on the physical side, not the mental.

You have to choose to spend hours and hours without moving.

You have to *want* to spend hours and hours without moving.

That's why most directors can't write, because to be a director you have to be the opposite of a slacker, in both the physical and mental sense.

The writer has to be a slacker physically, the opposite of a slacker mentally.

The director has to be the opposite of a slacker both physically and mentally.

A person who lives in motion, who needs to be in motion, is not a person who can write.

A person who is unable to spend hours and hours sitting in a chair, or lying on a mattress, or stretched out on a sofa, is not a person who can write.

I function as a screenwriter not because I'm a great writer, but because I'm capable of living in this basement.

The accumulation of hours in this basement is turning me into a good writer.

The accumulation of hours at the bar or the computer in my old lady's kitchen turned me into a decent writer.

When Santiago read my screenplay about the boy who throws his family into a well, he didn't read a good screenwriter, he read hours amassed at the computer in a small apartment kitchen.

Santiago kidnapped those hours amassed at the computer, and over time, he turned me into hours amassed in the basement.

I've improved a lot as a writer in this basement.

Santiago made me improve.

Santiago doesn't have the slightest idea what it means to write, but he does know how to improve my writing.

If this third screenplay ends up being the one that lets him film the movie that's going to change the course of world cinema history, it's going to be largely thanks to the basement, to the hours amassed in the basement (hours that continue to amass), and to Santiago.

*   *   *

Norma came down at three in the morning to bring me a cordless phone with Santiago's voice:

Pablo, I have good news. Very good news. Jack Nicholson is in. Meryl Streep and Jack Nicholson. Both without reading the script. My agent told me it's the first time he's ever heard of such a thing. He said maybe soon we won't even need screenwriters. Ha ha. I promised both Jack and Meryl that in a month I'm going to send them the first two acts, finished. In a month. A month, Pablo. It's now or never. Everything you've learned over the years, everything you are as an artist, has been leading up to this. Now or never. I'll be back in five days, and I'll be eager to read what you've written. I have a surprise for you. What? Yes, I'll be right there. Now or never, Pablo. Now or . . .

Norma yanked the phone from my ear and left.

I couldn't get back to sleep.

I spent two hours reading and rereading the scenes I've written since Santiago left.

I realized in horror that Jack Nicholson's character (a character who in my mind doesn't look anything like Jack Nicholson; he looks more like an overweight James Caan) has almost no lines.

His actions are essential, but he almost doesn't speak.

Maybe Jack will like that.

Jack?

Who the fuck am I to call Jack Nicholson *Jack?*

I would never have imagined, while I was watching *The Shining* in bed with my old lady, that someday I was going to write a screenplay for Jack Nicholson, that I was going to type words that Jack Nicholson would subsequently say onscreen.

Although the words I type aren't exactly the ones that Jack Nicholson is going to say onscreen.

Jack Nicholson is going to say the English translation of the words I type.

I actually have less than a month to finish the second act, because the translator is going to need several days to translate.

I don't know how long it takes to translate eighty pages of screenplay.

I'd like to meet the translator: the woman who translated Bolaño.

What's so special about that?

It's not like Bolaño was Arno Schmidt.

Any decent translator can do a decent translation of Bolaño.

Any decent translator can do a decent translation of our screenplay.

My screenplay.

I'd like to sit down to discuss the best way to translate my screenplay with the translator, but I don't speak English, or I speak very little, only enough to ask for a certain dish or to communicate with a stewardess.

I've just masturbated thinking about the translator: the first-ever professional translator who is also a sex bomb.

The final draft will belong to me and to Santiago and to the translator.

No, it will only be Santiago's, just as everything is only Santiago's in the end.

The whole world is going to end up belonging to Santiago Salvatierra.

I farted half an hour ago and I can still smell it.

The smell of my own farts turns my stomach.

The smell of my farts never used to turn my stomach, but now it does, today it does; I'm writing to distract myself and not let my turned stomach become retching.

I write I write I write.

I write the words "I write" while I write that I write the words "I write."

I've just fucked up.

My turned stomach went ahead and started retching, and I had to run to the bathroom and kneel in front of the toilet and vomit up this morning's fruit, and then, I don't know why, I opened the medicine cabinet and grabbed Volume III of Borges's *Complete Works* and I came out of the bathroom and tried to break the rectangle of light.

I hit the glass bricks over and over with Volume III of Borges's *Complete Works*, I really gave it to them with "The Book of Sand," with

"Shakespeare's Memory," but I couldn't break them; all I broke—mangled, ruined—was Volume III of Borges's *Complete Works*.

There's no way to fix it.

When Norma comes down she's going to see, and she's going to show it to Santiago, and I don't know what the hell I'm going to say when he asks me why I beat the shit out of Volume III of Borges's *Complete Works*.

Please Please Me is an album that puts me in a good mood, especially the song "Please Please Me."

I listened several times to the song "Please Please Me."

Lennon's voice fills me with the desire to live.

McCartney's, not so much.

*   *   *

I'm stuck; I can't move forward with the screenplay.

When I sit down on the mattress to write, I think about Meryl Streep and Jack Nicholson and the translator who is going to completely change anything I type, any word I use to build the scenes.

That's why I come to this encrypted file to write, because no one is going to translate this, no one is going to change it.

I'm afraid.

It's a fear I've never felt before.

A fear I don't understand.

It can't be fear of failure, because my reality as a basemented writer annuls the possibility of failure, the possibility that I will fail.

That's a lie.

I can't fail in the eyes of the world, but I can in Santiago's.

I'm afraid when I imagine what Santiago is capable of doing, of doing to me, if I fail.

That's a lie.

I can't stand the possibility of failing in my own eyes.

I have an opportunity that very few screenwriters have, that no Argentine screenwriter has ever had, and I want to make the most of it.

The problem is that the wish to make the most of the opportunity paralyzes me.

All the screenplays before this one (the one Santiago says is going to let him film the movie that will change the course of world cinema history), including the two I wrote for him and that he filmed in Spanish (one in Argentina, the other in Spain), were written without thinking about what was to come, in a kind of limbo made only of the present tense, with no room for the future beyond the notion that there was going to be a next day, and on that next day Santiago was going to read what I'd written the day before.

I miss that limbo.

I would give all the money Santiago never paid me to get it back.

I don't know why Santiago decided, for the first time ever, to give me hints about what's to come.

Is it because he feels insecure for the first time?

Or is it anxiety?

Or a strategy?

A new way of getting something out of me, something I didn't give him the last two times?

I don't know, but it's not working.

Knowing those actors, those Hollywood stars, are going to be in the movie Santiago will film with my screenplay killed my spontaneity and left me without an ounce of whatever measly bit of nerve I had.

Now everything I write seems calculated, every letter of every word of every sentence of every paragraph has a specific weight.

Every letter I type, I feel like I'm filling in the boxes of a word on an endless crossword puzzle.

I hate crossword puzzles.

Lisandro loves (loved?) crosswords; I hate them.

He could spend hours at a bar table with his *Quijote* magazines, filling in crossword puzzles (only crosswords, never word searches), while I read and reread Borges's stories and essays.

Lisandro would look at me with a smile every time he finished a crossword and he'd say, "I rocked it," and then start on another one.

I am far from finishing this crossword.

Today I read the two scenes I wrote yesterday, and when I finished reading I deleted them; I selected the two scenes, and without a second's hesitation, I pressed DELETE.

Then I tried to rewrite them.

I tried to forget about what I supposedly had to write, forget what our notes said should be written, but I couldn't forget.

Writing a good scene doesn't depend on forgetting the notes.

I didn't used to forget them, either; I simply settled them into a corner of my mind that allowed me to access those notes if I needed, but also to ignore them when necessary, to know the notes were there where I could see them out of the corner of my eyes, but to ignore them as I wrote.

Now the notes are in the center of my head; my eyes look inward and the first thing they see are the notes, written clearly, one after another, and, worst of all, they're in Santiago's handwriting.

This screenplay is not going to be better than *Amadeus*; it's not going to come within two meters of the quality, either structurally or scene by scene, of *Amadeus*.

But these days it's not necessary to write something as good as *Amadeus* in order to change the history of world cinema.

These days, the history of world cinema is changed with vulgarities—just look at the list of the most recent Best Picture winners.

These days, the history of world cinema is changed by failed movies, most of them vague, simplistic, with very little complexity.

The movies that win the Palme d'Or at Cannes, or the Jury Prize, are probably better than the ones that win the Best Picture Oscar, *much* better, but the movies that win at Cannes no longer change the history of world cinema.

Very few people care what happens at Cannes these days: just a small group of directors, actors, and writers in Latin America, Europe, and Asia who subsist by feeding off each other (I don't know if "feeding off each other" is the right phrase) like plant species on a permaculture farm; a group of directors, actors, and writers in Latin America, Europe, and Asia who form a social network that no one, or almost no one, cares about anymore.

That's a little over the top; what I just wrote is an exaggeration.

Or not so much.

I don't know.

It doesn't matter.

The only thing that matters is that I can sit on the mattress and type this, exaggeration or not, and not lose the habit of typing for several hours every day, because typing the letters that make the words that make the sentences that make the headings and actions and dialogues that form the scenes of this third screenplay is impossible.

*　*　*

Santiago came back with a huge amount of energy, a smile the size of the basement.

He brought me a gift: a vinyl copy of *Band on the Run* signed by Paul McCartney.

He told me that the night before he flew back here, he had dinner at Chateau Marmont with McCartney and his wife.

He told me Paul is a terrific guy.

The next day, one of the ex-Beatle's assistants showed up at his hotel (Santiago's) with two signed records (*Abbey Road* and *Band on the Run*) and a bottle of what, Santiago says, is a very expensive California wine.

While he was sharing the important news from his trip to Los Angeles, I was trying to understand why Santiago had decided to give me *Band on the Run* instead of *Abbey Road*: he knows the only thing I listen to is the Beatles, and that I never listen to solo albums by Lennon or McCartney or Harrison (I've told him more than once that I only listen to the Beatles), so why did he give me an album I don't listen to instead of an album that, in my opinion, is the second-best album in the history of pop music?

And in any case: Why did he tell me that in addition to *Band on the Run*, the record he planned to give me, he had also received *Abbey Road*, knowing that *Abbey Road* is much more important for me than *Band on the Run*?

He could have said nothing, kept *Abbey Road*, enjoyed it, and left me laboring under the conviction that the only record autographed by Paul McCartney that exists in this house in San Martín de los Andes is *Band on the Run*—a very good album, certainly, and a very good gift.

He asked me to show him the new scenes; his face full of enthusiasm, he asked me to open the Final Draft file and hand him the laptop.

He read the scenes with a serious expression that made my hands start to sweat; I couldn't stop wiping them on my sweatpants.

For five years now, I've worn nothing but round-necked T-shirts, sweatpants, and cotton socks.

Norma takes the bag with dirty clothes on Sunday morning, and comes down with the bag of clean clothes on Monday afternoon.

What is this? Santiago asked me.

He was looking at me with genuine confusion, and I thought I could see fear in his eyes.

It's all I've got, I told him.

Are you fucking with me?

No.

Three scenes. In ten days, while I was busting my ass in L.A. getting everything ready for this to be one of the best movies ever made, you wrote three scenes.

I wrote more than three.

And where are they?

I deleted them.

What?

I erased them. They didn't work. They weren't good scenes.

Are you fucking with me?

No.

Who are you to judge if those scenes were good or not?

The guy who wrote them.

He looked at me the way he looks at me when I answer him sarcastically, and he closed the laptop and threw it on the mattress.

How much is left in the second act? he asked.

I picked up the laptop, opened it, and showed him the Word file with the Aristotelian diagram of the screenplay; I had marked in red the plot point we had reached.

I felt Santiago's blood quicken: I could see Santiago's blood shaking him from inside like river rapids roaring through an ego-maniacal jungle.

I'm sorry, I told him.

I don't know why I said "I'm sorry."

He asked me to never again delete scenes, even if I think they're the worst scenes in movie history.

He told me that he will be the judge of our scenes, that he and no one else is going to decide from now on which scenes are useful and which scenes aren't.

He talked nonstop for half an hour, explaining why a writer must not be the judge of his own writings.

The writer does the work, he said, and doesn't judge. The artists are the ones who judge.

He told me that he is the artist, I am the writer.

Michelangelo was the artist, his assistants were the sculptors and painters.

He told me we couldn't fail his actors, that if they wanted to read the first two acts in less than a month, we had to send them the first two acts in less than a month, and if we fail in this then we're starting off on the wrong foot, and later on our Hollywood actors—our Hollywood stars—will make us pay for it; they'll keep quiet, days and days of silence, weeks, months, until they spit it back out in our faces when we least expect it.

Santiago always talks about *us* when he wants to convince me of something, or motivate me, or ask me to hurry up, although he's never asked me to hurry before now.

I asked him why he'd told me about the actors.

You never told me anything about the actors before, I said. At least not until everything was ready, a few days before you left to go film. Why now? Why did you tell me about Meryl Streep and Jack Nicholson?

And Sean Penn, he said.

What?

Sean Penn is in, too.

I wanted to break his face with a single punch.

I pictured myself breaking his face with a single punch, although I knew I wasn't going to move, I wasn't about to break any faces with any punches.

I realized that I found his head, completely bald except for the eyebrows, immensely annoying.

Again, I asked him why.

Because I believe in you, Pablo, he said. Because I know you are capable of writing an excellent script, the best script of all, with those actors in mind—the best actors in the world. You're ready. You weren't ready before, and now you are. I see it. I read it. It's harder, I get it, but the result is also going to be much more important. I'm giving you new condiments. Now go and cook up the tastiest stew in the world. A *locro* that will change the history of world cinema.

I didn't say what I wanted to say to him.

I never say what I want to say to him.

Santiago left and I had the words on the tip of my tongue.

I have to learn to interrupt him.

I have to learn to say what I think, without worrying about the consequences.

What can he do to me?

What do I have to lose?

I'm alone again, on the mattress, typing this instead of typing scenes, with more pressure than before, with less time than before, with my shirt soaked in sweat.

Two days passed and I didn't write anything, I couldn't even sit on the mattress to type bullshit in this encrypted file.

Day before yesterday, in the evening, I started to feel a slight pain on the right side of my abdomen.

A nuisance.

It's the first time I've felt it.

It must be my head.

My *head*, no: my mind.

Since I can't write, I invent pain.

I didn't say anything to Santiago, or to Norma, either.

When I woke up (I slept less than three hours), the pain was gone.

But last night, after dinner, it was back.

*   *   *

Santiago found Volume III of the *Complete Works*.

He asked me what had happened to Volume III, what I'd done to it, why it was semi-destroyed.

How'd you find it? I asked.

Doesn't matter how I found it, what matters is that I found it.

Santiago tends to say exactly the same thing when faced with similar situations, even if they're years apart.

He acts like an offended mother, a mother who is the world's worst mother but doesn't realize she's the world's worst mother, and who has the gall to get offended when someone does something that she doesn't look kindly on, something that is largely her own fault.

I lied to him: I said I'd tried to read Borges's Volume III, and that I'd gotten to the point where I felt a terrible anger, an uncontrollable anger, because of Borges, because I'd realized, all of a sudden, that one of the problems I have writing the scenes, ever since he told me about the translator, the woman who translated Bolaño, is that I write them in Spanish thinking in English, and everything sounds false, it doesn't matter that my English is very limited, I write in Spanish thinking that the Spanish is really a translation of English, and every word is a false word, just as many of Borges's words are false words, until in a fit I started to beat the volume against the wall, again and again against the wall, and—

Against which wall?

That one, I said, pointing to the wall opposite the rectangle of light.

Santiago looked at me the way he looks at me when he doesn't entirely believe me.

Don't lie to me, Pablo.

I'm not lying.

He looked at the door; he examined it, without moving.

Then he looked at the wall opposite the door; he examined it, without moving.

Then he looked at the rectangle of light; he examined it, without moving.

Then he looked at me, stared at me, into my eyes; he examined me a long time, without moving.

Then he looked at the semi-destroyed Volume III in his hands; he examined it, without moving.

Then he walked to the door, opened it, and turned around.

I'm going to order you a new Volume III from Librería Norte, he said, and he left.

*   *   *

Writing scenes is impossible.

I don't know how I was capable in the past of writing scenes.

I don't know how all the other screenwriters in the world manage to write screenplays, to finish screenplays that are subsequently filmed and transformed into movies that people go to the theater to see.

I'd like to erase everything I've written in this third screenplay, make it disappear, shake it off.

Start over with another story, different characters, without actors for those characters, without any production date.

I have to get back to my limbo.

I need my limbo.

How can I re-create it?

Even if it's a forced, artificial limbo.

I need Santiago to tell me the same thing my old lady told me when she realized that writing stories was important to me; I want him to come down tomorrow with my cup of coffee and little dish of fruit and tell me to take all the time I need, and then to leave me alone about the screenplay; I want him to tell me to forget about Jack Nicholson and Meryl Streep and Sean Penn, to forget about Hollywood, to write with the conviction that Hollywood doesn't exist as either a place or an industry, that it never existed at all; I want him to tell me I can take as long as I want, and that he isn't going to bother me, I want him to tell me to just let him know when I'm finished.

I read what I've written in this encrypted file.

I write that I read what I wrote in this encrypted file.

*   *   *

Santiago came down at five after seven in the morning and was surprised to find me working, freshly showered, rereading the first act and what we have of the second.

I asked him to leave.

He didn't understand.

I told him that if he wants me to finish the second act in time, I need him to leave me alone and not bother me until I finish.

He didn't like it when I said that.

He tried to convince me that it's better for us to keep going as we were, get back to our routine.

I told him the routine doesn't matter anymore, the routine is ruined, thanks to him, because he changed the rules.

He didn't like it when I said that.

He tried to convince me that the rules are the same, that all he did was give me a little more information, fill me in on details that he didn't fill me in on before, because I wasn't ready before, but I am now (same thing again: I wasn't ready before, now I am), he just wanted to make me a little more a part of the process.

I told him that I don't want to be part of any process that isn't writing, that I'm not interested in knowing about casting or locations much less budgets or crew, and much less than less about preproduction and production dates.

I told him that the only way to finish the screenplay is by ignoring those details, but that his presence, and the routine, do nothing but remind me of them, throw them in my face over and over again.

Let's do this, he said. Let's keep going as we were, but without talking any more about—

No.

I won't tell you any more details. Nothing. I'll come down same as every morning and we'll only talk about the script, about—

No.

He looked at me the way he looks at me when he thinks I'm behaving like an idiot:

Pablo, you can't ask me to—

If you don't do what I ask, this script doesn't get finished. I won't finish it. Finish it yourself if you want, but I'm not typing another word until you leave me alone. Stay upstairs listening to your autographed *Abbey Road*. Otherwise, no more writing gets done in this basement.

Pablo, please, listen to me, let's keep going—

Enough, Santiago. I'm not going to change my mind. Either you stay upstairs or the script doesn't get finished.

He pressed his thumbs against his eyes, and then he looked at me without blinking.

I thought he was going to pull the revolver from his waistband— I could see the butt peeking out.

He put a hand on my chest, his palm over my heart; in his eyes: a rage he could barely contain.

He didn't say anything, just picked up his chair and headed for the door.

Wait, I said.

He turned; in his eyes: a ray of hope shining through the rage.

Take the Borges volumes with you, I said.

Santiago left the chair on the floor, pulled out the revolver, and held it, without aiming it at me.

He opened the chamber and checked the number of bullets.

My hands produced liters of sweat; the cotton and polyester thighs of my sweatpants were soaked.

Two weeks, he said. I'll give you two weeks. Norma will bring down the food and leave. She'll open the door, leave the food on the floor, and close the door. Two weeks, so the translator will have seven days to translate it.

I nodded.

The finished script, he said.

No, I said, the first two acts. You said the actors are waiting for—

The finished script. In two weeks. I'll leave now and I won't come back until—he checked the calendar on his phone—Monday the twentieth. I want to see the word "FIN" at the end of the last page. Or if you want, you can write "THE END," so the translator has less work to do.

He went into the bathroom, grabbed the Borges volumes, put them on the chair seat, picked up the chair by its back, and left.

*   *   *

Two weeks.

One-third of the second act and the whole third act in fourteen days.

Impossible.

In the past three weeks I wrote four scenes, short ones, one of which shows one of the characters (Sean Penn's) going from one place to another in a brand-new convertible.

A three-line scene.

Three scenes and three lines in three weeks.

And now?

And now?

And now?

And now?

And now?

And now?

I'm going to sit on the mattress typing "And now?" in this encrypted file for the full two weeks.

How many times can I type "And now?" without going crazy?

I moved everything around: I put the mattress under the rect-angle of light, the shoebox against the wall opposite the door, I plugged the minifridge into the plug for the bedside lamp and the bedside lamp into the plug for the minifridge, put the stack of clean clothes next to the bathroom door, the bag of dirty clothes next to the basement door.

I sat on the mattress and opened the laptop.

It's strange not to have the rectangle of light across from me, and it's also strange to feel it above my head.

I thought about putting everything back where it had been.

For a long time, I sat there on the mattress, the laptop on my lap, thinking about putting everything back where it had been.

If I could write the screenplay the same way I write this encrypted file, completely unaware of what the next word will be, typing one word after another without worrying about the whole, without thinking about the context, the tone, the subject, the quality of the writing . . .

As Flannery O'Connor said: I don't know what I think until I read what I say.

I was tempted to ask Norma to bring down O'Connor's *Complete Stories*.

But if I asked Norma to bring down O'Connor's *Complete Stories*, I would probably spend hours reading them, convincing myself that the act of reading them counts as working on the screenplay, until night came and I realized that I'd typed little to nothing in the Final Draft file, and all I got from O'Connor's stories were healthy envy and pleasure.

What makes O'Connor's grotesque stories so fascinating is the presence of something larger than the characters that looms behind the characters themselves; in O'Connor's case, that something is the Catholic God.

I realized that the stories, novels, plays, and movies that I have most liked all tend to include the presence of something larger than the characters themselves looming behind the characters.

Amadeus includes that something, in the form—same as in O'Connor—of the Catholic God.

But that something larger than the characters themselves looming behind the characters doesn't have to be the Catholic God, or Allah, or Shiva; that something can be destiny, or a curse, or a center of electromagnetic energy.

In this third screenplay, the one that's supposed to change the course of world cinema history, the something larger than the characters that looms behind the characters is a movie.

The movie I am writing (trying to write) includes a movie, which in essence is the same movie that I am writing (trying to write), which is projected once a year in the basement of one of the characters' houses—Meryl Streep's—and that pushes the viewers toward a destiny they can't escape.

The destiny imprinted on them by the movie projected in the basement is much larger than any common destiny, fate, chance, or kismet.

I've just realized that the idea of the movie that determines the fate of the characters who watch it in the basement is pedantic, antiquated, half-assed meta-literature.

Meta-literature?

Half-assed postmodernism.

Postmodernism?

It's not an idea that can change world cinema history.

It's an idea of Santiago's I should have rejected the minute he brought it up, or at least called more vehemently into doubt; something good can sometimes come from a mediocre idea called vehemently into doubt.

How many times have I written the word "something" in this encrypted file?

When a writer who isn't a genius (who isn't Mozart) sits down with a laptop or a notebook to write the first thing that comes into his head, the words and linguistic constructions tend to repeat like crazy.

We writers who aren't geniuses are prisoners of those words and linguistic constructions.

I don't know if "linguistic constructions" is the right expression.

Our minds are locked in a prison of a limited number of words and linguistic constructions.

Five hours now I've been fighting the irrepressible desire to throw the first act and what I have of the second into the Recycling Bin, which on the MacBook Pro is called the Trash, and then empty the Recycling Bin/Trash.

If I stop writing in this encrypted file, there will be nothing left to do but throw the first act and what I have of the second into the Trash and then empty the Trash.

I also want to delete the file with the Aristotelian diagrams and the characters' backstories and the TextEdit file with the thousands of notes that Santiago unleashed into the basement's poisoned air and that we never used and that I don't plan to use even if Santiago comes down and spins the chamber of the revolver and aims at me and pulls the trigger fifty times.

Shivers of happiness run over my body when I think about eliminating all existing material related to this third screenplay I'm writing for Santiago Salvatierra, this screenplay that is supposed to change the course of world cinema history.

*   *   *

Norma brought me down a plate of *locro*, two slices of white bread, a glass of water, and three Red Bulls.

She was going to use the oxygen tank, but I told her there was no need.

I asked Santiago to ask you to leave the food by the door and close the door, I told her. And that's what I want you to do. Avoid coming into the basement as much as possible. I want no one in the basement.

She looked at me with what appeared to be a smile.

The first smile I've ever seen on Norma's face, though I'm not entirely sure it was a smile.

She left with the oxygen tank and closed the door.

Locro burns like hell.

I crawled to the nightstand and checked to be sure I had enough anti-hemorrhoid pills.

I forced myself to eat all the *locro* and the bread, and to drink all the water and one of the Red Bulls.

I sat on the mattress with the laptop on my lap.

I couldn't work.

I spent hours pacing the basement with the screenplay file open on the laptop on the mattress, the cursor blinking like a son of a bitch.

There was nothing to write.

I read the Aristotelian diagrams.

I read the backstories.

At two in the morning I read the TextEdit file with Santiago's notes.

The *locro* burbled in my stomach.

I drank another Red Bull.

There's nothing to type, I said to myself.

I picked up the ukelele and played a set of twelve Beatles songs that I learned in the past few weeks.

I had to learn them by ear, because Santiago never brought me the sheet music or lesson book for ukelele learners.

The ukelele is easy; it wasn't hard to figure out the most important chords, and I freestyled others.

"She's Leaving Home" is a McCartney masterpiece.

Too bad I can't sing.

I play the chords on the ukelele and whistle the melody.

Santiago told me the ukelele is really a ukulele; he said Santaolalla had informed him that it's really called a "ukulele," which in Hawaiian means "jumping fleas."

From that moment on he started to call it a "ukulele"; he even draws out the second "u" every time he pronounces the word.

But I can't bring myself to say "ukulele."

Or to write it.

And the strange thing is that Word shows "ukelele" as correct, not "ukulele."

Seems that Santaolalla is wiser than word processors when it comes to musical instruments.

The pain in the right side of my abdomen comes after dinner, almost half an hour later, and it lasts until morning.

Must be gas, monstrous farts that are blocking me up.

I used to shit every morning at seven, just before Santiago came downstairs.

Every day without exception.

Until Santiago stopped coming down.

It's been three days since I went to the bathroom.

That is, since I took a shit.

Why does "go to the bathroom" tend to mean "take a shit" and not "piss" or "shower" or "brush your teeth"?

People go to the bathroom for a wide variety of reasons.

Great songs have been composed in the bathroom.

Great novels have been written in the bathroom.

Maybe not entire novels, but chapters, yes, or paragraphs.

I used to correct my screenplays sitting on the toilet with the door closed, listening to my old lady in the kitchen typing emails on the PC.

She used two fingers to type.

Sometimes only one, when the other hand held the *mate*.

It's incredible how many things I can do in this basement other than write the screenplay I have to write.

* * *

Three days have already passed since I asked Santiago to leave and not come back.

I have eleven left.

Eleven days to write over a third of the screenplay that's supposed to change the course of world cinema history.

Over these past two days I've become convinced that much of what I've written needs to be rewritten.

I've even become convinced that I have to cut the idea of the movie that determines the destiny of the characters who watch it in the basement.

But if I cut that idea—an idea that is essential to the story we're telling, a mother-idea—I have to replace it with another, better idea that can be equally essential—another mother-idea.

I couldn't think of any other mother-idea that could replace the movie that determines the fate of the characters who watch it in the basement.

And if I do think of one, and if I put it into the screenplay, when Santiago reads it he'll probably blow my brains out for having wasted his time, for having cut his great idea, for replacing it with an idiotic and not at all essential idea.

What if I quit?

Is quitting a death sentence?

I can also spend these two weeks (that is, the eleven days I have left) masturbating, and then tell Santiago I didn't finish the screenplay.

Tell him that art—good art, anyway—is not something you can do in a hurry, not something you can schedule.

Tell him that just because Dostoyevsky wrote some of his novels in a few months, because he needed money from his editor to pay debts at the casino, it doesn't mean that all novels can be written in a few months.

There is no time in art.

Works are always being written, and rewritten, because they are imperfect, and an imperfect thing is also an unfinished thing.

Santiago abuses the word "perfection."

He believes he is a perfectionist.

He admires himself for always seeking perfection, even if in the process his production budgets double, and many of his collaborators, especially the actors, detest him with all their hearts.

Perfection doesn't exist.

Joyce's *Ulysses* is the best novel ever written, and it is a collection of countless imperfections.

I could ask Norma to bring it down, I'm sure Santiago has a copy of *Ulysses*.

Most likely he's never read it—tried, maybe, but never finished.

He probably felt confident when he started (just as most readers feel confident at first; Joyce was pretty clever starting out with such an accessible chapter), and then, as the prose grew more complicated, he probably ran out of steam.

Today I spent most of the morning thinking about Anita, the girl Santiago brought to the basement in my second basemented year.

A spider that was weaving a web above the rectangle's frame and that I didn't dare kill made me think of Anita.

I still remember her body, words, and face clearly.

A face much more perfect than Joyce's *Ulysses*.

Did Santiago lie to me when he told me Anita didn't want to come back, that she didn't like me?

Best to assume he lied.

What am I doing?

What do I gain by bringing Anita into this encrypted file, when what I need to do is finish writing a screenplay that's supposed to change the course of world cinema history?

I should delete this encrypted file, right this second, throw it into the Trash and empty the Trash.

Adios.

Unrecoverable.

Only the screenplay would remain, the Final Draft file with the first act and what we have of the second.

I should try to write the screenplay with the same freedom I have when I write in this encrypted file.

I wouldn't lose anything by trying.

Yes, I'd lose time, and I don't have much of that left.

Well, I also lose time typing in this encrypted file.

*   *   *

I've just realized I wasn't the one who asked Santiago to ask Norma to leave the food by the door and then close the door—it was Santiago's idea.

I told Norma that I asked Santiago to ask her to leave the food by the door and close the door, but now I remember it was Santiago's idea, I only asked him to leave me in peace, alone in the basement.

Santiago was the one who said Norma would open the door, leave me the food, and close the door.

I appropriated an idea of Santiago's, I made it mine with frightening ease.

I need to hear the rain.

That's the worst: depending on nature.

No one needs it to rain.

Except farmers.

Millions of people need it to rain.

Millions depend on nature.

But nature doesn't know how to write a screenplay capable of changing the course of world cinema history.

The rain doesn't know how to write a screenplay capable of changing the course of world cinema history.

The rain doesn't even know how to write *Pretty Woman*.

Santiago doesn't know how to write *Pretty Woman*.

I don't know how to write *Pretty Woman*.

Would Peter Shaffer have been capable of writing *Pretty Woman*?

It's much harder to write *Pretty Woman* than to write a screenplay that changes the course of world cinema history.

It's much harder to write *Pretty Woman* than *La dolce vita*.

I could pull a "Pierre Menard" with *La dolce vita*.

Anita had something of Estela Canto about her, or of a photo of Estela Canto that I found in one of the oh-so-boring Borges biographies.

Boring?

Who am I to say that Borges's life was boring?

Didn't Borges himself say that his life had been extremely boring, and that the life of an intellectual must be extremely boring?

At least Borges's life wasn't as boring as mine.

My biography is nothing but a sigh in a badly lit room of an abandoned fleabag motel in a town nobody cares about anymore.

My biography is the sum of still moments—holding a cup of

instant coffee with milk in my hand, watching through the window as biographies every bit as boring as mine pass by.

Moments with my old lady, having breakfast or lunch or dinner, in silence, or lying in bed and watching a movie, in silence.

A thousand-page biography, longer than Ellmann's on James Joyce.

Seven thousand pages, longer than Joseph Frank's five volumes on Dostoyevsky.

Full of moments that don't mean anything, or that mean very little.

A *Ulysses* composed of thousands of a single character's idle days.

Thousands of trips to the bathroom, sitting on the toilet with a story in my hand, a story I never once used to wipe my ass.

Thousands of scenes full of lines like:

"Pass the salt."

"Here you go."

"Thanks."

A naturalism of the most aberrant variety.

A seven-hundred-hour Lisandro Alonso film.

A biography worth nothing, until my trip to San Martín de los Andes, until my entrance into this shitty basement.

Santiago granted me an ending that breaks with naturalism.

Ending?

The sickening naturalism that was my life.

Sickening?

Sickening for the viewer, not for me.

There are no viewers of my Lisandro Alonso film.

There are no readers of the seven volumes, without photos, of my biography.

There are no readers of this encrypted file that I should throw into the Trash, just before I empty the Trash.

Or are there?

Is Santiago the reader of this encrypted file?

Can Santiago connect wirelessly to this MacBook Pro, *his* Mac-Book Pro, and read what I'm writing?

If that's the case, though I doubt it (best to doubt it), I'll dedicate a few lines to you here, Santiago Salvatierra:

You don't know how to write.

You don't know how to write.

You don't know how to write.

You don't know how to write.

You don't know how to write.

You don't know how to write.

You don't know how to write.

You don't know how to write.

You don't know how to write.

*   *   *

Now Norma knocks on the door before she opens it; she waits for me to knock on my side before she opens the door, leaves the food and water, and then closes it.

Santiago took my proposal seriously, and he's going to leave me alone, *alone* alone, in the hopes that I'll finish the screenplay once and for all.

The first draft.

Then he's going to give me his notes, and he'll ask me to make the corrections in one day.

I'm not going to have time to contradict his notes, to kill them without his realizing I'm killing them: a skill I mastered while writing the second screenplay.

Directors don't like it when you say no to them.

I only know one other director besides Santiago, but I have no qualms about stating that directors, whatever part of the world they come from, don't like it when you say no to them.

When you say no to one of their ideas or notes, they'll likely dig their heels in about that idea or note, even if they have their own doubts about it.

It's also likely that, after receiving a couple of nos, they'll start compulsively rejecting every one of your ideas and notes.

Several times I saw in Santiago's eyes that he liked one of my ideas, that it had even surprised him, and a few seconds later, unable to help himself, he'd say:

No, Pablo, that's crazy. No one in real life would do something like that.

But movies aren't real life.

That's why most movies based on real lives don't work.

Movies are movies, and it doesn't matter if they're original ideas or not, based on real lives or not.

When someone sits down to watch a movie, they *watch a movie*, and they enjoy that movie or they don't, it doesn't matter whether it's an original idea or not, whether it's based on real lives or not.

Biopics don't work.

Except *Amadeus*, which isn't a biopic.

Peter Shaffer used characters that really existed in order to talk about the struggle between the artist and his irrevocable mediocrity.

No one who sees *Amadeus* thinks that it really happened, that the events they're watching are true.

Viewers shouldn't care where the movie comes from, they should only care about the movie.

How many times have we seen movies that don't work, and then someone comes to its defense by saying, "But it's a true story," or, "That really happened"?

A lot of ideas that come from real life don't work in movies.

As screenwriters, we have to forget that certain ideas came from real life, forget the notion that because something really happened, it must be respected.

There is nothing that must be respected when it comes to writing a screenplay.

The movie exists in its own reality, and that reality is the only one that should matter to us.

A reality constructed of elements that are real, but that we also invent.

That we invent completely.

Norma is part of Santiago's invented reality.

Most likely, I am also part of Santiago's invented reality.

Maybe the entire world . . . no, the entire *universe*, is part of Santiago's invented reality.

The basement has smelled like *locro* for two days straight now.

Today I drank four Red Bulls.

I did push-ups for an hour—tomorrow my arms are going to hurt like hell.

The pain in the right side of my abdomen comes and goes.

When it comes, it lasts for two or three hours.

Usually, I feel it coming on little by little, and I try to ignore it until it becomes impossible to ignore, and then I let it be, I convince myself that the pain is going to last forever, and after two or three hours it goes away.

The bass line of "Getting Better" is better than all the screenplays ever written; all screenplays in all languages, the screenplays that were produced and the ones that were abandoned.

I stood for an hour under the rectangle of light, the sun on my face.

I don't know if it was for an hour.

I had lunch standing under the rectangle, a turkey sandwich with cheese and tomato, a little mayo.

I've told Norma several times that I like my sandwiches with more mayo, but she doesn't hear me, or she ignores me, or she thinks that amount of mayo is a lot of mayo.

Have they given me up for dead in Buenos Aires?

Do they give a disappeared person up for dead?

How long does a person have to be gone before they're given up for dead?

Did they look for me?

Did the police come from Buenos Aires to San Martín de los Andes?

Did they talk to Santiago?

Was there some witness who saw Santiago pick me up at the Chapelco Airport?

Would the police care about finding a fortysomething man who doesn't have a job or a bank account or a credit card and who doesn't pay taxes and who lives with his mother in an apartment in Belgrano?

Did my old lady come to San Martín de los Andes?

Did she walk through the quaint little dirt streets hoping to find me?

Could she have crossed paths with Santiago's four-by-four?

Did she come alone, or with Lisandro?

Lisandro listened to Pink Floyd nonstop.

I listened to the Beatles, he listened to Pink Floyd.

Hundreds of hours of discussion.

I'd tell him that Pink Floyd's biggest problem was that they took themselves too seriously, and he'd say that the Beatles' biggest problem was that their passion for rebellion had kept them from ever leaving childhood behind, and I'd tell him that that was one of the Beatles' virtues, that the biggest problem with many artists, not just musicians, was that they were no longer children.

The Beatles were Joyce, Pink Floyd was Sábato.

The Beatles understood that melody was more important than experimentation; that way of understanding art should be applied to screenplays: the story with its plot, conflict, climax, and falling action must always be more important than the visual or narrative experimentation.

Santiago is Pink Floyd, though he thinks he is the Beatles.

Santiago doesn't seem to worry much about his image; he shaves his head completely bald and he always wears green—green shirt and green pants and green socks, no brands, no logos; sometimes he wears jeans, sometimes sweatpants of a soft, semi-shiny material.

One morning he came into the basement in pleated green pants and a green short-sleeved shirt, and I asked him why he wore so much green.

He told me it was the only color that didn't bore him.

Green is a color that stops being a color after a while, he told me. It's a color that I tend to avoid in my movies, in the color design of my movies. I tend to avoid trees. When you film in towns or cities, you have to avoid trees. In spring and summer, at least. Trees bring a romantic warmth to the locations, a warmth that is usually at odds with the characters' emotional state, with the emotional state of the world, this world we live in. But green is also a color I like to have around, in real life.

Santiago's movies (the ones that came before this one that I have to finish writing in seven days, this one that's supposed to change the course of world cinema history) tend to tell the stories of marginal characters, characters who've been pushed to the margins of society.

Santiago tells the stories of the neediest.

He lives in mansions and stays in sumptuous hotels, and from that palatial conglomerate of enormous houses and presidential suites scattered over a large portion of the globe, he tells the stories of the neediest.

Santiago is addicted to didacticism, he imagines that his movies are parables; he is convinced that his art makes the world a better place.

*   *   *

I feel more and more strongly (I grow more convinced by the hour) that the only way to finish this third screenplay is by starting it over from scratch.

The pain in the right side of my abdomen intensifies as I grow more convinced that the only way to finish this third screenplay is by starting it over from scratch.

It's impossible to write the entire screenplay of a movie that will change the course of world cinema history in one week, and yet, that's the only way to write this one.

Santiago won't be able to stand it when he finds out that his screenplay changed entirely.

Unless the new screenplay is stunningly good.

It's impossible to write a stunningly good screenplay in seven days.

During their first years as Beatles, Lennon and McCartney composed a song a day; Harrison and Ringo came to the studio without knowing those songs, and they had to improvise the arrangements as they were recording, which they did with nerve and joy.

If I had a bit of the nerve and joy that Harrison had in 1964, maybe I'd be capable of writing this screenplay in seven days.

No, the problem isn't a lack of nerve, or nerve and joy; the problem is that I'm not a genius.

You have to be a genius to compose an album as good as *A Hard Day's Night* in one week.

You have to be a genius to write a screenplay that changes the course of world cinema history in one week.

And I am not a genius, that much is abundantly clear.

I have a little talent, and the ability to work for many hours, and to use those hours to carry out the most unpleasant part of writing—the structuring, the diagramming and all that.

I compensate for my limitations with hours worked.

And as I've said, when it comes to writing, Santiago is no genius, either.

He doesn't even have talent.

He doesn't even have the ability to work on the scenes for hours and hours, because he gets distracted easily; his body asks him to move, his body and mind ask him to get out of the basement and get to directing.

Santiago the writer is a kid with a slight (or not so slight) mental disability.

No, not even, because a kid with a slight (or not so slight) mental disability at least has innocence, and innocence can be a great advantage when one sets out to write.

Santiago is a kid with a slight (or not so slight) mental disability who is convinced he is a great writer.

A kid with a slight (or not so slight) mental disability who struts around the world with the self-importance of Henry James.

*   *   *

Meryl Streep in a green room, wrapped in a green cassock, looking at the camera and reciting the lyrics of "I Am the Walrus" over and over for ninety minutes.

I am the egg man, they are the egg men . . .

Andy Warhol could have made that movie, and he would've been called genius.

In today's Hollywood, if someone tried to make a movie like that, if they presented the idea of making a movie where Meryl Streep, in a green room, wrapped in a green cassock, looked into the camera and recited the lyrics of "I Am the Walrus" over and over for ninety minutes, most likely they'd ask him to leave and shut the door on his way out.

The system that rules Hollywood is rigged against art in cinema.

"Art" is a synonym for "incomprehensibility," which in turn is a synonym for "failure," which in turn is a synonym for "few tickets sold."

This screenplay that I have to finish in the next seven days, or rewrite entirely, has to be a screenplay that Hollywood accepts with open arms.

It has to be an oxymoron: a work of art that Hollywood accepts with open arms.

I don't think Santiago knows what an oxymoron is.

*   *   *

Five days.

No, four days and twenty-two hours.

I don't know how many minutes.

Minutes don't matter.

Minutes don't count when you're writing.

Days and hours.

Norma brought me a beef *milanesa* with mashed potatoes smothered in Mexican *salsa verde*.

I thought about telling her about the pain in the right side of my abdomen.

No, the pain doesn't exist.

A pain that comes and goes doesn't exist.

A real and true pain never goes away.

This feeling is of something rotting inside me.

The screenplay.

The screenplay is rotting inside me.

The screenplay that I should be writing, that I should be molding into scenes in the Final Draft file.

A screenplay that is a child with a degenerative disease who for some reason they've stopped medicating.

A sick kid abandoned to his fate.

Can you die from a rotten screenplay?

Such a shame, his screenplay just went bad inside him, they didn't catch it in time.

*   *   *

I've just done something crazy.

I woke up with the urge to write.

It's been months since that happened.

Over coffee, I read the first act and what we have of the second act of this third screenplay, the one that must change the course of world cinema history.

I chugged a Red Bull.

I ate three little cubes of apple.

I reread the first act and what we have of the second.

I closed the screenplay file.

I closed my eyes.

I opened them.

I closed them again.

I ate two little cubes of melon.

I moved the screenplay file into the Trash.

I closed my eyes.

I opened them.

I chugged another Red Bull in one gulp.

My heart beating as fast as it could.

Few times in my life have I felt such excitement.

The pain in the right side of my abdomen came and went; it came, a few seconds, it went, it came back, a few seconds, it went, and . . .

Empty Trash.

Letters the size of the basement.

No, of San Martín de los Andes.

Letters the size of Neuquén.

I closed my eyes.

Opened them.

A square of pineapple.

I closed them.

Opened them.

I emptied the Trash.

I spent a long time trying to find out if it's possible to recover files that were thrown into the Trash just before emptying the Trash.

Nope.

At least, I can't figure out how to do it, and without internet I can't google it.

I could ask Norma to ask Santiago to google it.

I don't want to think about Santiago; I've just betrayed him, I've just deleted months of work, I've just deleted three-fourths of a screenplay that could have changed the history of world cinema.

As Santiago said: Who am I to judge what can or can't change the history of world cinema?

He's the one with all the awards.

He's the one who knew how to become the greatest Latin American film director of all time.

Who am I to make a decision like that?

It's done, I already made it.

The screenplay doesn't exist.

That is, part of the screenplay exists on the external hard drive and in the printed scenes that Santiago hasn't shredded yet, something he usually does after we move the notes handwritten in the margins of the A4 pages into the Final Draft file.

It bothers me to know that an old version exists on the external hard drive, and I'm sure that Santiago also downloaded it to his computer, so it exists on the external hard drive and on Santiago's computer, or only on Santiago's computer, since he's probably used the external hard drive to store other things, I don't know what, it doesn't matter what, all that matters is that I know that the old version isn't even half a screenplay, fifty-something pages that I have to forget.

I have to forget *everything*.

Anything that concerns this third screenplay.

The acts and scenes and characters with their backstories and the Aristotelian diagrams.

I have to forget it all and destroy it.

Destroy the forgetting.

Fail in the most terrifying way.

Fail and accept the failure and tremble in fear until I find the door that's not completely closed and that will allow me to start over.

Let Santiago come on Monday and see the failure and kill me
with a bullet between the eyes.

Goodbye to the terror.

Goodbye to the pain in the right side of my abdomen.

They're going to belong to someone else.

To a self who no longer matters.

A disappeared, dead, finished self; that is, my true self.

A self that is the *I* that I should be.

Now.

Start to *be* the I that I've been for five years now, though I didn't
want to admit it.

*   *   *

It was a mistake.

Deleting the file with the first act and what we had of the second
didn't accomplish anything.

There are three days left and I haven't even written a heading.

Scene Heading

INT. BASEMENT—DAY

I couldn't even bring myself to open a new file.

I spend my time stretched out on the mattress, belly up, using
the laptop's clock to measure how many minutes the sun lasts in
the rectangle.

How easy it is to waste time.

If a guy could get paid for doing nothing . . .

Movie actors are paid fortunes for largely doing nothing.

They spend ninety percent of the workday not acting.

True, they do get up early.

A car goes to pick them up at the hotel, or the rented apartment, or
their house if they're lucky enough to shoot in the city they live in, and

it takes them to the set or location; one, two, or three hours of makeup; they drink coffee while the crew lights the scene; they live in the trailer, fucking off with the endless technological fuckeries that were surely given to them as gifts (movie actors tend to charge really high fees, but they never pay for anything, it's all comped), at most memorizing their lines for the day, usually a scene that is no more than three pages long.

If people got paid for doing nothing, my old lady and I would have been millionaires.

*　　*　　*

INT. BASEMENT—NIGHT

The wee hours of the morning.

My old lady must be snoring peacefully.

Does she take sleeping pills?

Has she recovered her calm after my disappearance?

Did she lose her calm after my disappearance?

My old lady snores in a way that isn't annoying; her snoring even helped me fall asleep, it relaxed me, slowed my thoughts.

It's impossible to get a mind full of thoughts to sleep.

Does she snore, or *did* she snore?

If my old lady is dead, then the bullet between my eyes will take me to her.

To where?

There's nothing after this.

It's ridiculous to think there is.

This is all there is: the screenplay, the unwritten screenplay.

Santiago is going to have a stroke when he finds out I threw the screenplay in the Trash and emptied the Trash.

Maybe he'll know how to recover files after they were thrown into the Trash and the Trash was emptied.

No, better not to recover it, start from scratch.

Three days.

An act a day.

Write a full-length screenplay the way Kerouac wrote *On the Road*: an unbroken stream, no paragraph breaks.

Let the woman who translated Bolaño take care of organizing the text.

Scene heading, action, character, parenthetical, dialogue, transition, heading, action, character, parenthetical . . .

On the Road is an overrated novel.

Though I never read the original.

Maybe the editors ruined it.

In the United States, writers collaborate a lot with their editors; much more than in other countries.

I don't know what I'm saying.

I'm not saying anything, I'm *writing*.

I don't know what I'm writing.

No one knows what I'm writing.

This encrypted file is never going to be edited by a literary editor.

Paragraph break.

I feel like the paragraph break is necessary, it helps keep the eyes and the mind from running on.

The mind gets tired of running on.

The mind gets tired of writing bullshit in this encrypted file, when what it should do is write the screenplay.

The mind gets tired of doing what it shouldn't be doing when it knows that what it should do is something else.

Open a new Final Draft file and:

EXT. WASHINGTON SQUARE—DAY

I'm going to ask Norma to ask Santiago to buy me some Don DeLillo novels.

DeLillo writes the best sentences in world literature.

DeLillo started to write later in life, like me; he was even older when he started, close to thirty; he said he only realized he *could* write (that writing was a discipline to which he could dedicate himself) when he was halfway through his first novel.

Did I just compare myself to DeLillo?

Santiago is correct: I should never have taken up writing.

It's all my old lady's fault.

Why that computer?

She could have designed her web page and checked her emails at an internet café.

The apartment had no room for a PC.

That machine, if it hadn't been for my obsession with writing a story a day, would have spent most of its time asleep, doing nothing, taking up space in a kitchen that barely had enough room for us to move between the table, the counter, the stove, and the fridge.

Did my old lady intuit, when I suggested we buy the PC, that I would end up using it for something more useful than music?

Anything other than music.

The impossibility of comfortably moving around in the kitchen instead of music.

*   *   *

I've just learned a quite respectable version of "Happiness Is a Warm Gun."

Happiness is Santiago's revolver with a single bullet that yanks me from this basement forever.

No, that yanks me from the responsibility of writing the screenplay, the fucking screenplay that has to change the course of world cinema history.

Who cares about world cinema history?

How many fuckers study film history in a given year worldwide?

Changing the course of world cinema history today doesn't mean anything for the world.

Art no longer changes the world the way it used to, the way Joyce did with *Ulysses*, or Beckett with his trilogy that isn't a trilogy.

World cinema history of the past two decades is just a brief epilogue in film history books.

The past two decades take up no more than five pages, no photos, no footnotes.

*   *   *

Locro again.

Santiago must have the idea that I write better when I fill up with gas, that I float around the basement with the laptop hanging from my neck.

But it's only the farts that float, that try to escape, that know what's coming before long . . .

It's impossible to write a screenplay in two days and change.

Better not to touch the *locro*.

I have to be sure that the pain in the right side of my abdomen isn't gas.

I'll go on a fast.

I won't eat anything until Monday, when Santiago comes down with his chair and the little dish of fruit.

I dumped the *locro* into the toilet and flushed.

I poured the Red Bulls into the toilet and flushed.

Nothing but mineral water until Monday.

Today is Friday, almost Saturday.

*   *   *

INT. BATHROOM—BASEMENT—NIGHT

I took a shower sitting on the toilet.

If I'd had them, I would have dried off with Borges's *Complete Works*.

Did Santiago order Volume III from Librería Norte?

Most likely, on Monday he'll come down with all four volumes and the chair and the little dish of fruit and the cup of coffee and the revolver loaded with six bullets.

Or he'll never come down again.

Maybe Santiago ditched me but didn't want to go through the awkward moment of actually ditching me, so he's going to keep me locked down here while he goes and works with another screenwriter.

Norma is putting poison drops in the *locro*, and in the Red Bulls.

A poison meant to kill me slowly, without my realizing it.

Maybe the pain in the right side of my abdomen . . .

The pain started before I asked Santiago to leave me alone.

I'm not sure that it started before.

Yes, it started before.

There is no other screenwriter.

Santiago doesn't have time to pick up the screenplay with another writer, especially not his fifty-something-page version.

Although Santiago could have the most recent version.

He's probably taken it wirelessly from this laptop.

Santiago can probably connect wirelessly to my brain.

Not my brain, my mind.

Maybe he was taking the scenes from my mind without my realizing it.

That's why I can't find them.

Like in Cronenberg's movie *Scanners*.

Santiago can't stand Cronenberg; he almost died when he found out Cronenberg won the Special Jury Prize at Cannes with *Crash*.

Telépatas: Mentes destructoras.

Telepaths: Destructive Minds.

They destroy English titles in Spanish-speaking countries.

If I remember correctly, *Crash* in Mexico is called *Extraños placeres, Strange Pleasures*.

Dead Ringers: Pacto de amor, Inseparables, Mortalmente parecidos, Gemelos de la muerte. Pact of Love, Inseparable, Deadly Similar, Death Twins.

I don't know why I remember that kind of bullshit.

Santiago usually gives his movies titles that don't need to be translated.

A single, universal word.

*   *   *

Two days.

Less than two days.

I haven't written a single action.

Yesterday at dawn the pain in the right side of my abdomen came to stay.

I just fucked up big-time.

Norma knocked on the door, waited for me to knock from my side, opened it, came in with the breakfast tray, and knelt down to leave it on the floor; I asked her to bring it closer to the mattress,

I told her I was tired, that I'd spent the whole night writing and I couldn't move, and unfortunately she complied.

She came over to the mattress with the tray: scrambled eggs and a sausage covered in Mexican *salsa verde*, a bottle of mineral water, a little dish of fruit, two Red Bulls.

She knelt down to set it beside the pillow, and, in a rapid movement, I grabbed her tit.

I squeezed, not too hard.

Norma took a second to react.

She grabbed the revolver, but didn't aim it at me.

The tit didn't feel like a tit.

A balloon full of water that's been deflating for years.

A testicular sac without testicles, filled with water and sand . . . no, milk and sand . . . whole milk.

In her eyes: surprise.

Surprise that didn't last even five seconds and was quickly replaced by a front of calm, a calm full of hatred, an ocean of calm that vibrated with the shock waves of a tsunami of hatred.

She tried to take my hand from her tit.

She couldn't.

I asked her if she wanted to lie down with me.

Just for a while, I told her.

She took a step back, my fingers clutching her tit.

She hit my wrist with the butt of the gun.

It didn't hurt.

The pain in the right side of my abdomen annuls all other pain.

I realized I'd gotten hard.

Very hard.

I thought about lowering my sweatpants to show her.

She aimed at my face.

I didn't let go.

The rectangle was darker than usual, a black window, a black frame with glass someone painted black.

Norma took another step back and I let her go.

Without moving from the mattress, I said I was sorry.

She did not forgive me.

She kept the gun aimed at me.

I told her I didn't even want Red Bulls for breakfast, I told her to take it all, except the mineral water.

She put the revolver in her apron pocket, picked up the mineral water, and walked to the door.

No, I said, not the water. Leave me the water and take the breakfast and the Red Bulls.

She unscrewed the water bottle's cap and took a long drink.

Then she opened the door and left, taking the last ounces of mineral water with her.

I examined the breakfast on the tray.

The cup of coffee tempted me: one good cup of coffee before dying.

I emptied a can of Red Bull in the toilet, flushed, and filled the can with tap water.

I don't like tap water.

*   *   *

If a drunk, bored genie trapped in a magic lamp no one had rubbed in centuries were to escape, appear before me now, and grant me the wish to be a musician, any musician, I would choose to be Prince.

That is, insert logo of the Artist Formerly Known as Prince.

Prince sweated music, shat music, even his toothbrush against his teeth had rhythm and melody.

Probably the all-time best guitarist of rock, pop, funk, and soul—a guitarist who tried to imitate his favorite singers' voices with his guitar.

I could never imitate Peter Shaffer with my words.

I've tried.

I tried many times.

But luckily I didn't waste much time before realizing that Peter Shaffer is playing a different sport, or the same sport but in a different category, and that I'd best stick to trying to be a top ten player in my own category: "mediocres under thirty" when I started, "passables under forty" when I wrote the screenplay about the boy who throws his family into a well and the first two screenplays for Santiago; "good but blocked under fifty" at this precise moment, while I type these pointless lines in a pointless encrypted file.

How much time is left?

I want it to be Monday.

Now.

Let Santiago come down with his revolver.

Now.

Prince, or the Artist Formerly Known As, composed almost forty albums.

Actually, he composed more than forty (that is, he had enough songs for fifteen hundred albums), but he released almost forty, which is still a monstrous number.

At the Buenos Aires School of Music I had a professor who adored Prince, or the Artist Formerly Known As, more than he adored his five-year-old son; he talked only about Prince, or the Artist Formerly Known As, all the time about Prince, or the Artist Formerly Known As; he compared everything with Prince, or the Artist Formerly Known As, and everything came up short against Prince, or the Artist Formerly Known As.

He had tried, ever since he was nine years old, to play the guitar like Prince, or the Artist Formerly Known As, and at twenty-eight he had realized it was impossible—even if he practiced eight hours a day (which he did, Monday to Sunday)—to play guitar like Prince, or the Artist Formerly Known As, and he accepted his life as a professor at the Buenos Aires School of Music.

I don't remember his name.

I'm really bad with names.

I was always bad with names.

I'd be introduced to someone, and I'd say hello to him or her and offer a few words of small talk, and the name would be erased from my mind; then I'd spend all my time looking for subtle ways to make the person say their name again.

On the other hand, I never forget a face, not even the ones I'd like to forget.

I remember in detail the faces of all the women who went out with me and who for various reasons decided to stop going out with me, and the faces of all the women who went out with me and for various reasons I decided to stop going out with.

I remember in detail the faces of all my classmates in grade school, high school, and at the Buenos Aires School of Music.

My teachers, too, the ones who liked me and the ones who didn't, though most of them liked me, not because I was a good student (though I *was* a good student), but because I wasn't one to break their balls much.

*   *   *

Push-ups till I'm exhausted.

The pain in my triceps was my excuse not to write.

Nor could I masturbate.

I could barely lift the can of Red Bull and take a sip of water.

Now that my arms hurt a little less, instead of writing the screenplay that's supposed to change the course of world cinema history, I'm writing this in the encrypted file, knowing that in a day and a half this fucking farce is over.

Suddenly, this file shines with the importance of a last will and testament.

My final words.

I shouldn't have done push-ups till I was exhausted, now typing is torture.

I'm exaggerating.

Having your fingernails ripped out with pliers is torture.

Typing is annoying; every time I hit a key I feel a slight pain in my forearm and triceps.

If I'd buckled down, in these five days in the basement I could have worked out each and every one of my muscles, without weights, using only my bodyweight.

I could have asked Santiago to bring down the external hard drive full of exercise videos for working different muscle groups, and also for stretching them, because if I didn't stretch I would have ended up stiff as an old man with multiple sclerosis.

It's impossible to play the ukelele with tired arms.

Not impossible, but it's hard.

A while ago I thought about using GarageBand to record a sung version of this encrypted file.

I'm going to ask Santiago to sit in his chair and listen to the entire file, in its ukelele and voice version, before he puts the bullet between my eyes.

No, I'm not going to record anything.

It would end up being a piece of shit, and I would erase it, just like I should erase this encrypted file.

Throw it in the Trash and empty the Trash.

I should open an unencrypted Word file and write a letter to my old lady, ask Santiago to print it and send it.

My old lady wouldn't have liked it if a genie turned me into Prince; she would have preferred Spinetta.

She would have been happy with Luis Alberto Spinetta for a son.

According to her, he was the only Argentine who was really worth anything, the only Argentine in history who would have been worth cloning.

Utopia is a country populated only by Spinettas.

Anti-utopia is a country populated only by Santiago Salvatierras.

And the Salvatierras declare war on the Spinettas.

And the Spinettas don't have the slightest chance fighting in hand-to-hand combat against the Salvatierras.

The existence of two countries populated only by Santiago Salvatierras would mark the beginning of the end of the world.

A world that for a while now has deserved to be split in two by a meteorite, this time one the same size as the Earth.

Two Earths crashing into each other one Monday morning, leaving only dust, without Spinetta's music, without Salvatierra's images.

Or let the same meteorite that made the dinosaurs disappear do the same with the Santiago Salvatierras who wander the Earth convinced that it was created for them alone.

I envy the people who go through life as if the Earth had been created for them alone.

I envy them and I detest them.

And I detest my envy of them.

It's impossible to possess something you can't even fully encapsulate.

Spinetta's lyrics hide the secret of eternal life.

May the bullet between my eyes turn me into a Spinetta lyric.

*　　*　　*

Writing in this encrypted file, I've learned to type with my eyes on the screen; I don't look at the keyboard, and I make almost no mistakes.

I could get a job as one of those typists who sits next to the judge during trials and types everything that is said.

What are those typists called?

Do they use those typists in Argentina?

I don't know what I'm writing.

I was never good at research.

I'm too lazy.

I can spend hours and hours writing or diagramming, but I get bored after a few minutes of researching.

In the screenplays I wrote at home on the computer in my old lady's kitchen, when I found myself faced with the need to research some aspect of a scene's action or one of the characters' professions, I used to use common sense, consult the trove of information I'd collected over years of watching movies and TV shows and reading books, and write the first thing that came to mind.

Later, as the internet grew, I'd google the information and copy it exactly.

I plagiarized Wikipedia almost as much as Foster Wallace plagiarized DeLillo.

Since I've been in the basement, since I've been collaborating with Santiago, we have (he has) a group of researchers living who knows where who take care of our research.

They send us files in English and Spanish with the specific

information meticulously organized and clearly explained, with photos that have detailed captions.

Santiago calls that group of researchers living who knows where "the Group."

"I'll ask the Group to check it out," he says.

Research is the worst thing about writing screenplays.

Research is the worst thing about writing anything.

The pain in the right side of my abdomen is starting to feel like a knife.

A dull knife with a rounded point that's being used to spread butter over my appendix or gallbladder.

The kind of pain you want to press and probe.

I flipped through the *Playboy*s for an hour: none of those women look like Norma.

I'm going to cover the holes in the basement and leave the shower on.

I'll tell Santiago there's been a flood, that a pipe must have burst, I was asleep and didn't realize, the laptop's ruined.

We lost everything. Everything, Santiago.

Although he probably knows someone who can fix it, who can recover the supposedly irretrievable data from the hard drive.

He'll find my encrypted file, and he'll unencrypt it.

I have to unencrypt it myself, take it out of the Utilities folder in Applications and place it in the center of the desktop.

This encrypted file is my testament.

Let Santiago read it after he kills me and decide what to do with it.

Hopefully he'll print it and send it to my old lady.

Hopefully he'll read all the way to these final lines and he'll print the file and mail it to my mother.

UNENCRYPTED WORD FILE

Gallstones.

Pebbles.

Ideal for playing jacks, or *payana*—a game originally called *kapichua* and played by the Toba and Wichí peoples with pits or seed, a game that helped them develop manual dexterity and learn to count.

I don't know where I got that information.

The bus's speakers are blasting Prince, or the Artist Formerly Known As: "Starfish and Coffee."

I'm writing this in an unencrypted Word file on the 15-inch MacBook Pro.

I stole it from Santiago's house, from his second-floor study with its view of trees and sky.

I also stole the crossed-out notebook, *my* crossed-out notebook, which Santiago had kept in his library between Volumes I and II of Borges's *Complete Works*.

I have about twenty hours left in the trip, in my semi-sleeper seat.

I've realized that the black marks in the notebook are not as thorough as I thought; with a little patience, you can see through them to read what I wrote.

When I realized you can read what I wrote, I felt afraid.

Here on the bus, I can't read because it makes me dizzy.

I can write, but I can't read what I write.

I never really knew what it is that keeps me from reading in cars and on buses.

A problem with my eyes?

With my brain?

With my stomach?

One page is enough to send me running to the little bathroom to throw up.

A tray with two sandwiches, a flattened brownie, oily cheese, and *dulce de batata*; Cepita orange juice; Villa del Sur bottled water.

The bus is full.

The person in front of me leaned his chair back as far as it goes and barely left me room to open the laptop.

When I turn my head to the left, the landscape tries to convince me that we're in the Swiss Alps.

I know that the closer we get to Buenos Aires, the more the landscape will fall to pieces; it will flatten and grow depressed to the point that it'll be best not to look at it, not even out of the corner of my eye.

*   *   *

I knelt down next to Santiago's body and checked his neck and wrists for a pulse, trying not to look at his exploded head.

I couldn't help it: the gelatinous hole in the skull, the spattered brains on the smooth cement floor and the walls.

Dead.

No pulse.

No images.

The mineral water is warm, almost hot; they must have accidentally left the bottles in the sun before loading them onto the bus.

The sandwiches are edible: cooked ham, cheese, and butter—very little butter.

At least they don't burn like Norma's *locro*.

Like all of Norma's dishes.

Chile poblano and cilantro.

Never in what remains of my life, if I have any life remaining, will I ever eat Mexican food again.

I shaved with Santiago's razor: I cut off my beard with scissors and then I shaved.

Not a peep from Norma.

I bought the bus ticket using the name Santiago Salvatierra; I have his ID and his credit card.

I was afraid that if I said my name, alarms would go off.

What alarms?

My name must have already been erased from the registers.

My name only exists in my mother, if my mother still exists.

It exists in Lisandro, if Lisandro still exists.

Maybe it exists in Anita, if Anita still exists.

I don't think it exists in Norma, though Norma does exist; I left her in the house, sitting in the chair that Santiago used to bring down to the basement, in the kitchen, rubbing her legs as if she were freezing cold.

I asked her what she was going to do.

She didn't answer.

I thought about apologizing for having disrespected her during these past months, the months that Santiago spent preproducing our third movie—the one that had to change the course of world cinema history—and then shooting it, postproducing it, and promoting it.

*   *   *

Santiago came down Monday morning as he had promised, with his chair, a cup of coffee, and a little dish of fruit.

He set the chair against the wall, under the rectangle of light, and examined the basement.

Then he came over to where I was, sitting on the mattress, the laptop on my lap, Bose headphones over my ears (the Beatles' complete discography on shuffle at top volume), left the cup of coffee and dish of fruit on the floor, and said something that I didn't understand.

A girl in the seat behind me is tapping her fingernail against the window glass.

I don't know if bus windows are made of glass.

Plasticky glass.

Glassy plastic.

I think I'm going to close the laptop and go on writing in the crossed-out notebook.

A fourth of the notebook has clean, perfectly lined pages just waiting for me.

Did Santiago read it?

I don't have a pen.

I'll borrow one.

What am I going to do when I get to Buenos Aires?

I'm going to buzz the intercom, and my old lady is going to open the door for me, and she's going to give me a long hug, and we're going to take the elevator to the fourth floor and walk down the hall to apartment 4B, and open the door, and go inside, and sit down at the kitchen table with a *mate* that we'll share in silence, and after a while I'm going to give her forehead a kiss, and she's going to prepare another *mate* for me, and we're going to lie down on the bed to watch the movie that was supposed to change the history of world cinema, a pirated copy that I'll buy in Retiro.

I want to turn around and see the girl.

She got onto the bus after I did; I didn't see her, I was too obsessed with convincing myself that it was impossible to read what I'd written in the notebook through the marks.

I couldn't convince myself.

I guess in the lousy light of the basement the marks seemed more thorough.

F. Murray Abraham is a despicable person.

I'm going to get up to go to the bathroom so I can sneak a look at the girl.

I hate bus bathrooms, even more than I hate the bathrooms on airplanes, and one of those bathrooms killed my old man, broke his neck.

I stay in my seat, typing on this laptop.

An unencrypted file, on the desktop, that I called Journey.

The encrypted file is still in the same place, in the Utilities folder in Applications.

I don't know if Santiago read it.

I didn't find any changes in the text.

The last sentence ("Hopefully he'll read all the way to these final lines and he'll print the file and mail it to my mother.") is still the last: the final words I wrote in the encrypted file before the frenzy.

It's hard to type looking only at the screen.

The bus shakes like hell.

I type looking at the keyboard, and then I glance at what I wrote, and correct it quickly.

If I stop to read what I wrote, I get dizzy.

And if I get nauseous, I'm not going to be able to keep writing.

And if I don't write, then I don't have anything to do.

Listen to the Beatles, again the Beatles, without headphones, forcing the rest of the passengers to listen to them along with me.

I should have brought Santaolalla's ukelele.

Ukulele.

I wasn't thinking very clearly, shall we say, during the minutes after Santiago's death.

* * *

Right now, as I listen to the girl's fingernail against the plasticky glass or glassy plastic of her window, I'm wondering whether Norma has a family.

Why would a person agree to leave her country to live as a maid in the house of a crazy egomaniac at the ass end of the world?

Did Santiago pay Norma a salary that she sent to her family in Mexico?

Why did Norma let me go?

How can someone live so far from the people she loves the most so she can send them money—that is, take care of the people she loves the most, but without having them close by, without even seeing them?

Hopefully Santiago's will stipulates that everything he has (had) should go to Norma; not to his idiot son, Hilario, but to the self-sacrificing Mexican maid who planted hemorrhoids in my ass and watered them every day with her demonic potions.

* * *

We just stopped at a Shell with a minimart.

I used Santiago's card to buy a bag of Lay's potato chips, three Rhodesias, a chocolate Cachafaz *alfajor*, a liter and a half of Sprite, two Pico Dulce lollipops, and an XL River Plate sweatshirt that I hope will keep me from shivering so much every time they crank up the air conditioner.

I should have set the basement on fire with Santiago still inside, erased all the evidence.

I should have become Santiago.

Shaved my whole head.

No, let my hair and beard grow until they covered me.

Sunglasses.

I should have learned English, and when I reached Los Angeles said I'd had a hair treatment, that I'd felt the need to change something about myself after my last movie.

I can't be Santiago.

Am I going to miss his skeptical nights?

Am I going to miss the basement?

Am I going to miss the basement more than I miss my old man?

What am I saying?

Not *saying*, *writing*.

I'm going to miss my life in the basement because it's probably the only life that . . .

I should have stayed, died of starvation beside Santiago's body.

Coagulated blood.

Santiago sausage with *chile poblano* and cilantro.

*　　*　　*

The first week in the basement without the laptop was interminable.

I spent it playing ukelele: a set of twenty-five Beatles songs and "Plegaria para un niño dormido" by Spinetta.

I sang at the top of my lungs.

That is, I yelled the songs.

I strummed the strings with rage.

The fourth one broke on me.

High G.

I learned to play with three strings.

The ukelele is an instrument it's hard not to fall in love with.

Every time Norma came in with my food, I was afraid she would take it away from me, that she'd hand me the phone with Santiago's voice and I'd hear:

Santaolalla needs his ukulele.

But Norma never handed me any phone.

The ukelele was my only companion during the nearly two years it took Santiago to preproduce, shoot, postproduce, and promote the movie that was supposed to change the course of world cinema history.

The ukelele and the *Playboys*.

And the minifridge that held the bottles of mineral water and the fruit I didn't eat at breakfast.

And the mattress.

It makes me sad to think about the mattress: poor worn-out mattress, my brother-in-arms.

When it wore out I started to sleep better, almost as well as if I slept on the floor.

Three nights of smooth cement and goodbye, back pain.

I couldn't find the Bose headphones in Santiago's study.

I bought some cheap ones in the Shell minimart, the only ones they had, Califone brand.

They sound like shit, but they sound.

A little better than *like shit*.

Lennon is singing "Come Together."

George Martin with Califone earphones: he'd jump off the Tower of London.

I could travel to England, see Liverpool, the Cavern Club,

London, Abbey Road Studios, I could walk down Abbey Road listening to the Beatles, only the Beatles, always the Beatles, in my Califone earphones.

The bus's air conditioner is going to make me catch a cold.

I should have bought two River sweatshirts, one to use as a scarf.

There was no air-conditioning in the basement.

In the summer, the cuboid of poisoned air turned into a sauna.

I spent the whole day naked, except when Santiago came down with his chair, the cup of coffee, the little dish of fruit, and the printouts with his notes.

At first I also put on clothes when Norma brought the food down or came in to clean, but then I stopped bothering, I stayed undressed, usually just in my underwear, watching Norma as she leaned the bag of clean clothes next to the bathroom door and took the dirty clothes away.

In summer, in addition to his chair, the cup of coffee, the little dish of fruit, and the printouts with his notes, Santiago would sometimes, on days when the heat was most suffocating, come down with a portable Daitsu air conditioner.

One morning I asked him if he would lend me the air conditioner for a few days, but he said no.

It uses too much electricity, he said. It's crazy how much power these gadgets use. And here in San Martín the electrical system is a disaster. You've got to be careful and not overuse it. It's boiling hot upstairs, too, but better that than end up in the dark.

It's not easy to spend three months with your balls constantly sweaty.

I used to touch them without thinking, and when I unconsciously brought my hand to my face, the smell practically broke my nose.

*   *   *

I'm listening to "Ob-La-Di, Ob-La-Da."

Life goes on brahhh, Lala how the life goes on.

Good thing the Beatles weren't born in Spain, or Latin America.

For lyrics to work in Spanish, they have to be semi-incomprehensible, like Spinetta's.

I wish I had some Spinetta albums on the laptop.

I could turn and ask the girl behind me, or any of the other passengers.

Someone must have a Spinetta album, or at least a song.

I'd also need a USB drive.

Santiago smiled with his whole face when I handed him the laptop and he read "THE END" at the end of the Final Draft file.

He had no idea what came before that.

Not even *I* had any idea.

Although I could sense it: the best screenplay I'd ever written.

I looked on the laptop for the screenplay, the one that was supposed to change the course of world cinema history, but I couldn't find it.

Santiago erased it.

He erased everything, except the encrypted file and the Beatles albums.

I forgot the *Band on the Run* vinyl autographed by McCartney.

I could have stolen the signed *Abbey Road* from the second-floor study.

Did I see it?

I didn't see it.

Today's Paul McCartney isn't the same as the old one.

Is today's Paul McCartney even Paul McCartney?

When John Lennon died, Paul McCartney ceased to exist.

When Santiago Salvatierra died, Pablo Betances ceased to exist.

I went to see McCartney at River Stadium with my old lady

(how long ago was that?) and we were bored to tears by that band of millionaire geezers who were as far away from Abbey Road as we were, the nobodies sitting on the grass.

My old man was a fan of Cuarteto Cedrón; I don't know if he was a *fan*, but he listened to them a lot, especially the album with poems by Raúl González Tuñón.

I miss my old man.

I can't remember his face, but I miss him.

I remember Spinetta's face, but not my old man's.

Spinetta y los Socios del Desierto.

My old man with Spinetta's face.

Though my old man never wore sunglasses.

I could use some sunglasses now: the guy in front of me has the curtain on his window open and the sun shines right in my face.

I could turn and ask the girl behind me if she'll lend me her sunglasses.

I don't know if she has sunglasses.

I don't know if she has eyes.

Norma, sitting in Santiago's chair in the kitchen, did have eyes.

Old eyes.

I talked to her, I told her things, but she didn't answer.

I asked her if she had anywhere to go.

She didn't answer.

She'd taken off her apron.

I think.

No, I'm sure.

A flowered dress.

A dress made of material for cheap curtains.

I put on a pair of Santiago's Nike sneakers that I found in a closet under the stairs.

They're too small for me.

I can't figure out why I need to write this.

I did understand it in the basement (I think I understood), but not here, on the bus, now that I'm free.

Free?

Does some part of me imagine that this is publishable?

Is this the way I'm choosing to return to life: become a crossed-out notebook, exist in the near future as an encrypted file that, in the twists and turns of life, some publisher will end up printing?

Is my hope of becoming a published book real?

No.

I write because it's all I know how to do.

The only way to exist when you don't exist.

When I stop typing on this laptop, I'm nothing.

I'm going to write on the laptop and in the notebook at the same time.

First in the notebook, then I'll copy it to the laptop, and while I copy it, I'll correct it.

No, to copy from the notebook to the laptop I have to read, and I can't read.

Better to go on like this, typing like a bored chimpanzee (not bored, *desperate*) that someone, for some reason, taught to type.

*   *   *

I made a mistake.

An unforgivable mistake.

I shouldn't have stolen Santiago's credit card.

When the police investigate his death they're going to find the charges with the bus company and the minimart.

But how will they know it was me?

What am I going to say when I return to life?

Will I tell the truth?

No one will believe me.

I don't even have the last screenplay on the laptop to somehow imply that I wrote it.

No digital trail.

The police are going to find proof of my stay in the basement; hairs from my head and beard and legs and balls; hair surrounding Santiago's body.

I'll wait for the police to find the proof and come for me, and I'll spill the whole story.

No one will doubt that I wrote the screenplays once they find out about the atrocity.

Even those who doubt will say they don't.

The film world is going to talk about this atrocity.

The world of world cinema.

I'll become a symbol.

The subjugated artist.

No, *exploited*.

The nameless writer who is now finally baptized while the whole world looks on.

Pablo Betances, Argentine, screenwriter, atrocity victim.

The writers guilds will all honor me.

I'll travel the world from homage to homage.

The Writers Guild of America will grant me the title of honorary member.

Free medical coverage for me and my old lady.

And for my wife.

I'll go back to San Martín de los Andes and look for Anita, take her with me to Los Angeles, to New York, London, San Sebastián.

Fox Searchlight will produce the screenplay about the boy who throws his family into a well.

A cascade of praise.

No critic will be able to write a bad review of my movie once the atrocity is known.

The best actors in the world will kiss my feet.

The *Hollywood Reporter* will talk about the kidnapped writer.

Honorary doctorates from Harvard and Yale.

Honorific degree from the University of Buenos Aires.

Horrorific degree.

Dresses worth a thousand, two thousand, three thousand dollars so my old lady and Anita can shine on the red carpets of Cannes, Venice, Berlin, the Golden Globes, the Oscars.

My old lady on my right and Anita on my left, second row of the Dolby Theatre, behind Meryl and Jack, in front of Sean, Tom, Leo, Angelina.

They'll strip Santiago of his awards for best screenplay and they'll bestow them on me in emotional ceremonies, my old lady crying with happiness, Anita taking her by the arm . . .

No, Norma will incriminate me, she's going to twist what really happened.

A crazy fan who spent years chasing him, Santiago Salvatierra's very own Mark Chapman.

I should have stayed in the house, talked to Norma, convinced her of the atrocities that Santiago committed against both of us, I should have made her part of my atrocity and me part of hers, made it *our* atrocity, the two of us cellmates.

I swear I'm not going to tell them anything, Norma. I promise you. No one is going to find out.

*   *   *

I've just asked the driver to turn down the air conditioner.

He didn't look at me, just made a gesture with his right hand that I didn't understand.

The copilot or codriver sleeps in a little cabin above the first row of seats—I saw him get in there a while ago: he took off his sneakers and left them on the floor, next to his seat.

I could switch them with my Nikes, which are tight in the arch and the toes.

I don't know why I don't take them off.

I closed the laptop, put it between my hip and the armrest, took off my sneakers, stored them under the seat, opened the laptop, felt the cold on my feet, closed the laptop, put it between my hip and the armrest, took my sneakers from under the seat, put them on, opened the laptop.

Norma must be setting Neuquén on fire.

Or else she strapped on Santiago's skis and went up to Chapelco.

I've never skied.

Lisandro invited me to Bariloche with his family once, but I couldn't be bothered to take a trip like that just to spend my days watching them slide down Cerro Catedral, while I followed behind an instructor teaching wedge turns on the bunny slopes around the hotel.

If I open the curtain on my window the sun will warm me up a little, but I won't be able to see what I'm writing.

Turn the brightness all the way up.

It's not enough.

The laptop doesn't have much battery left, and this ancient bus doesn't have electrical outlets.

Nineteen percent.

The battery on this old MacBook Pro isn't what it used to be.

I'm going to type until it runs out, then I'll open the curtain and enjoy the sun and write in the crossed-out notebook.

I hear *la gorda* Serra Lima playing over the bus speakers.

My grandmother, my old man's old lady, wore out her Serra Lima albums; a visit to her was a visit to *la gorda* (as she called Serra Lima).

I could have played Norma a few *rancheras* on the ukelele, softened her up with her own music.

I don't know any Mexican *rancheras*.

A little of "El Rey":

Con dinero o sin dinero, hago siempre lo que quiero, y mi palabra es la ley.

"With or without money, I always do what I want, and my word is law."

My word is law in this unencrypted file.

During my years in the basement Santiago's word was law, except in the crossed-out notebook, and later in the encrypted file.

The words I wrote in the screenplays were Santiago's.

Words that I wrote, I typed, I invented, words I pulled from some part of my mind, my heart, my stomach, but that were Santiago's.

Santiago Salvatierra invented Pablo Betances in the basement.

He invented everything I was in that basement, except for the crossed-out notebook, except for the encrypted file, except for the screenplay I wrote in full that day between Sunday afternoon and Monday morning, those pages I wrote in one sitting, all the way to the end, when I typed the words "THE END," two words that are really one—"*FIN*"—at six forty-eight in the morning, twelve minutes before Santiago would come down with his chair, the cup of coffee, and the little dish of fruit.

A screenplay that I don't have.

A screenplay that is a movie I didn't see.

A screenplay that, to tell the truth, I hardly remember at all.

*   *   *

I don't know if it's right for the driver to play music over the bus's speakers, for him to impose his music on us.

Gilda's *Greatest Hits.*

I put in the Califone earphones, opened iTunes with the Beatles discography, then the White Album disc two, then "Helter Skelter" at maximum volume, but in the end I had to pause because behind McCartney's cries, I could hear Gilda's tropical murmur.

It's worse to listen to an amalgam of the Beatles and Gilda than to listen just to Gilda.

Gilda has some good songs.

The producer who worked on her albums was apparently deaf in at least one ear, but I like the songs, and Gilda's voice sounds honest and not too pedantic.

I should have stayed at the Buenos Aires School of Music, finished my degree.

What difference does age make?

How many of those kids who played instruments as if they were natural extensions of their bodies ever made names for themselves as musicians?

I didn't give myself a chance to find out what my ceiling was.

I imagine my ceiling wasn't very high, true, but maybe it was a unique ceiling, special, mine; a ceiling other musicians could have wanted as a shelter for their songs, their albums, their concerts.

The truth is, I never felt like a musician.

I enrolled in the Buenos Aires School of Music because music was what I liked most in the world, but I never imagined myself living the life of a musician.

I tried to convince myself that, yes, a musician's life was the life for me, but I don't think I was ever convinced.

A serious musician doesn't live with his mother.

A serious writer, yes (Borges, for example), but not a musician.

Was it my obsessive reading of Borges's *Complete Works* that gave me the idea that I could live with my mother for what remained of my life?

What remained of my life?

I don't remember ever thinking that, imagining the possibility of living with my old lady for what remained of my life.

I never thought about my life beyond a month into the future.

Not even a month—fifteen days.

Even in the basement, when I understood that imprisonment was the only possible life for me, I didn't think beyond two or three days.

Sometimes not even that; hours—the future was made of hours.

Am I going to miss the stillness of the basement?

The solidity of a routine I managed to get used to.

Not only did I get used to it—I enjoyed the routine, I respected it, revered it.

A routine that was a ritual.

All my life I lived from routine to routine, from ritual to ritual.

I abhor people who live in the moment, those fake Buddhists, and real Buddhists, too.

I don't abhor them, I envy them.

The ones who improvise a new life from one day to the next.

It bothers me immensely that those people exist.

My future as a musician was a farce, a delusion born out of believing I was something I'm not.

My old lady understood, when she heard me discuss my musical dreams, that it wasn't a life for me; her subtle—or not so subtle— attempts to pull me from my musician's path were desperate attempts to save me.

I should have become a monk, imposed a religion on myself, any religion, and locked myself away in a monastery or temple, where I'd live by an extremely strict routine that's been perfected over the course of centuries, centuries of repetition.

The basement was my monastery, my temple.

An indispensable ritual to avoid writing like shit.

There is no serious writer who doesn't live by some sort of ritual—self-imposed, learned, imitated, or plagiarized.

I am capable of loving a ritual, a routine, more than I love a person.

I would marry a beautiful routine, form a family with three little ones, three little routines whom I would watch grow up slowly, educate with pride and patience, in a pretty house in La Lucila, not too big but comfortable, with enough room for my four routines to develop to their fullest potential.

Routine equals *happiness*.

A static, negligible happiness, but happiness nonetheless.

People who live in motion find moments of happiness: a much more intense happiness, but one that doesn't last long.

Santiago was one of those people who never stopped moving.

Santiago was not a happy person.

In all the time we spent together in the basement, I never saw him give off even a glimmer of happiness, not even when he came down to tell me about everything we had won, or everything *he* had won, with our movies, his movies.

Was Norma happy living with Santiago?

A horrible happiness, but happiness nonetheless.

Not much more horrible than my happiness in the basement.

If only Norma had been less fiendishly pigheaded and agreed to say one word to me, talk to me . . .

Only once did I hear her voice: one afternoon, Santiago and I had gotten caught up in an argument about the possibilities for the reversal of a scene, and Santiago threw in the towel, picked up his chair, and left the basement, and he passed Norma on her way down to bring me lunch, and I heard them speak to each other; I couldn't hear the words, but I did hear Norma's timid voice, her sweet and funny Mexican accent.

The landscape has started to flatten.

The first cows have appeared, grazing and shooing flies.

The cows graze and shoo.

They shoo grazing.

They graze shooing.

It wouldn't surprise me if I found out (that is, if someone else found out and told me) that cows live in the most absolute happiness.

Norma has the eyes of a cow.

A cow capable of the most shocking cruelty.

The Aztec Hera.

At first the revolver in the pocket of her maid's apron made me laugh, but then I realized Norma carried that revolver with the utmost ease, that she wouldn't hesitate one second to use it, and that she would do it swiftly.

*   *   *

INT. BUS—DAY

The girl in the seat behind me taps a fingernail against her window to the beat of "Macarena."

How do I know it's a girl?

I didn't see her get on.

She hasn't said a word.

Is it from the way she moves and breathes?

Breathes, no; *sighs*.

It's impossible to hear the different ways the passengers breathe;

Gilda devours the sound, Gilda and her band, but you can hear bodies sliding in seats, along with sighs, coughs, throats clearing.

I type this and eye the battery percentage every five words.

Five percent.

Santiago asked me how it had gone with the script.

He looked tired, a little sad.

I thought about asking him what was wrong, if everything was okay with Hilario, or with the actors, or the financiers.

I told him things had gone well.

Very well, I said.

You finished it?

Yes.

And?

I don't know, read it.

He saw something in my face that he didn't like.

He asked me to hand him the laptop.

He sat in his chair, the laptop on his lap, and he smiled when he saw the words "THE END"; at least, I assume it was that two-word word that made him smile.

Then he moved the cursor to the first page and started to read.

I spent the day before Santiago came down to the basement—with his chair, the cup of coffee, and the little dish of fruit—doing nothing, trying to convince myself that the pain in the right side of my abdomen was only an invention, a psychological pain that grew at the same rate as the impossibility of writing the screenplay that had to change the course of world cinema history.

I was never much of a hypochondriac.

I figured it was a lesson in the mind's ability to invent pain, aches that are real and hurt but don't have a physical cause; they're in the body but don't belong to the body, they belong to the mind.

Wrong: when I woke up from the anesthesia, they told me that my first-ever invented pain had not been invented.

I invented that the pain was invented, and I convinced myself of that for too long.

Is general anesthesia necessary to remove gallstones?

Four percent.

It was six in the afternoon when the guilt kicked in.

Guilt and shame.

Guilt, shame, and anger.

Guilt, shame, anger, and a tremendous urge to cry.

Or rather, the tremendous urge to cry was the result of the guilt, shame, and anger.

And hatred.

Hatred for my decision to have writer's block.

Decision?

No one decides to be blocked.

It was the pressure that blocked me.

The pressure that was a gift from Santiago: a package the size of Neuquén that held a golden statuette he brought from L.A.

That's a lie.

At six-oh-five in the afternoon I had already discerned the enormous lie.

Had I really been blocked?

If I'd had writer's block, would I have been able to write in the encrypted file?

Yes, because writing in the encrypted file, or in the crossed-out notebook, or in this unencrypted file, or very soon in the notebook again, is not writing.

There are great books of world literature that were not written, that are not literature.

Malone Dies, for example—the novel I read more times than

any other, the novel I would take to a desert island if I were such a moron as to go to an island with only one book.

A novel that is not a novel.

Literature that is not literature.

A book that was not written.

Those are usually the best books: the unwritten ones.

But it's impossible to write a screenplay without writing.

It's impossible to be blocked if one is not writing.

Beckett could not have been blocked writing *Malone Dies*.

He could have had writer's block writing *Endgame*, or *Play*, or even his last works like *Company* or *Worstward Ho*, which are extremely planned texts, with quiet, precise staging.

Three percent.

The Gilda album ended, and no other music came on to replace it.

The girl taps her fingernail against her window to the beat of Mozart's "Eine kleine Nachtmusik (Serenade)."

Ta, ta ta, ta ta ta ta ta ta, ta, ta ta, ta ta ta ta ta ta.

I imagined greeting Santiago Monday morning and telling him I hadn't written anything, that not only had I not written anything but I had deleted what we had, I'd thrown it into the Trash and emptied the Trash.

I saw myself telling him that, saying words that didn't belong to me, that could not belong to me, because a mediocre writer, a drudge writer, doesn't have the right to be blocked, doesn't have the right to throw the screenplay into the Trash and empty the Trash, he doesn't have the right to utter those words.

Who the hell am I to have writer's block like that?

I urgently needed to shit, and I rushed to the bathroom, to the toilet, but I didn't have much to expel, so mostly I expelled gas.

I thought that the pain in the right side of my abdomen would go away after that cascade of gas, but no, it got sharper, more pointed, and then I told myself that maybe the only way to get rid of the pain in the right side of my abdomen, the only way to throw it in the Trash and empty the Trash, was by trying to write: sit on the mattress with the laptop on my lap and try to write the screenplay that was supposed to change the course of world cinema history, from the beginning, from "FADE IN:" to "THE END."

Two percent.

I should have gone to one of the more luxurious bus companies, bought a ticket for a VIP sleeper seat that reclines all the way, with classical music, electrical outlets, hot food.

Why this uncomfortable semi-sleeper?

I didn't want to call attention to myself.

Whose attention?

I guess one of the things that most seduces me about *Malone Dies* is the way Beckett attains such vast depths using the simplest words; the text is always there, within reach, but at the same time it escapes us; we understand everything, but we have to read and reread to truly understand.

In screenwriting, you must always use simple words.

Explain.

A screenplay is a text that has to be quickly understood.

The fewer secrets there are between the writer and the reader (that is, the producers, actors, directors of photography, costume designers, technicians, etc.), the better the screenplay.

The screenwriter who tries to demonstrate what a good stylist he is while writing a screenplay should be thrown into a well and abandoned to God's wrath.

I'm going to try to sleep for a while.

I'd trade in my Califone earphones for a pair of earplugs.

The fingernail against the plasticky glass or glassy plastic is going to drive me crazy.

Turn and say something to her.

No: poor girl, she needs to tap her fingernail against the window in order to endure the trip.

We all need such activities to endure the hours: typing bullshit in this unencrypted file, or tapping a fingernail against the glass, or picking a booger from a nostril and analyzing it for a while to decide whether it's worth eating or not.

My nostrils could hide an exact copy of the meteorite that extinguished the dinosaurs.

Actually, if I were such a moron as to go to a desert island with only one book, I would take *Ulysses*.

A person could spend a lifetime reading *Ulysses* and only *Ulysses*, but I don't know if you could spend a lifetime reading *Malone Dies* and only *Malone Dies*.

Ulysses never ends; I liked to read it as if it were a deserted beach where I could swim anytime I wanted, knowing that the water lapping my feet was different every time.

Ta, ta ta, ta ta ta ta ta ta.

Mozart was the kind of genius worth calling a *genius*.

These days, they call anyone a *genius*.

The constant, desperate search for artistic geniuses.

The problem is that if we start to call artists *geniuses* when they aren't, then the new generations learn to see them as geniuses, and they imitate them, and then over time the geniuses who deserve to be called *geniuses* disappear, because we're used to calling those who aren't geniuses *geniuses*.

It's absurd to compose music after Mozart.

Absurd to write after *Ulysses*.

Absurd to make movies after Tarkovsky.

One percent.

I tore out a page from the notebook and ripped it in two, stuck half in my mouth, chewed it and spit it out, and improvised an earplug for one ear; then I did the same with the other half.

*   *   *

The bus's only TV (a cube full of circuits for which replacements no longer exist) has just come on.

After a few seconds of almost black gray: color lines, the Universal Pictures logo, the Amblin Entertainment logo, and then the beginning of *Back to the Future*.

A much more difficult film to write than *La dolce vita*, much, much more difficult than *Fitzcarraldo*.

A masterwork of entertainment.

How many rainy Saturdays and Sundays did I spend in bed watching *Back to the Future*?

How many rainless Saturdays and Sundays did I spend in bed watching *Back to the Future*?

This trip to Buenos Aires is my *Back to the Future*.

I'm going back in time, to what I had before, to what I was before (although I don't know if I still have or am anything from that past), to live it in the future.

An extremely boring *Back to the Future*.

Nothing further from entertainment than my past life that I'm trying to return to.

An independent film applauded only by the director's friends and family.

A movie that no studio or producer wanted to fund, that only got made thanks to the support of the director's millionaire uncle, who in reality used his nephew's film to launder money.

I'm an unfunny Marty McFly.

A Marty McFly who agreed to be kidnapped, who agreed to be exploited for years, and who made no attempt to escape.

A Marty McFly who travels to the future in the least exciting time machine in the history of world cinema.

*   *   *

That Sunday afternoon in the basement, when the guilt and shame and anger started to shake me (my body simultaneously stock-still and shivering), each and every one of the ideas in the screenplay that was supposed to change the course of world cinema history struck me as the very worst idea, the structure as the very worst structure: an enormous Aristotelian diagram that may have made the old Peripatetic proud, but that simply didn't work . . .

No, it wouldn't have made Aristotle proud, it would have made him start shouting the same curses that my old man shouted at the duty-free shop employees when he found shooting the shit like useless cows, or even more useless than cows, because in the end no one is going to want to toss any of those duty-free shop employees on the grill.

I sat down to write it.

I said to hell with Aristotle and I sat down to write the screenplay that had to change the course of world cinema history.

I sat on the mattress, back against the wall, laptop on my lap, and, as I had done that first time with Mann's *Magic Mountain*, I started writing by plagiarizing, but this time I was plagiarizing myself, typing the same heading I'd used to start the first act of the now deleted draft, and then I typed the first paragraph of action, and I stopped, and I read and reread those words I knew by heart, and I imagined them in English, I couldn't help it, and I decided in that precise moment that the only way to write that screenplay, the one that had to change the course of world cinema history, the only way to write it and finish it, was by rewriting it without rewriting it, transforming what I already knew of the story into scenes, but forgetting about the preestablished structure, the diagrams and backstories and piles of notes, un-Aristotling the story, un-Aristotling myself, succumbing to the immediate, only the immediate, without letting

UN-CROSSED-OUT NOTEBOOK

I slept for almost three hours.

I'm writing this on the un-crossed-out pages of the notebook, peeking every once in a while at the blah and un-poetic fields of La Pampa.

I don't know if we're in La Pampa.

Whatever, it's all the same out there.

I'm going to ask the driver to stop, and I'll get off, walk to one of the farms, and beg to be hired as a farmhand.

I don't know much about farmwork, but I can learn, focus on one discipline and not stop until I master it.

A more dignified way to suffer abuse, and one with a nobler purpose: to bring forth food from the earth.

A useful, essential purpose—much more worthwhile, useful, and essential than writing movies, or writing anything.

Frenzy.

That's the only word for what happened in the basement that Sunday afternoon/evening and early Monday morning.

The sentences appeared in my mind at an exorbitant speed, they surfaced like bubbles in a glass of soda.

My fingers were bewildered, they tripped over each other as they typed, but I didn't stop to edit, fuck editing (this is a screenplay, I repeated to myself in the gaps between words and sentences, not a work of literature), no one cares *how*, focus on the *what*, only the *what* matters, the *what what what*.

The *what* came over me, from inside out, and took control of my hands.

If someone were to tell me that in the hours I spent typing like I was possessed my face bore no expression other than the feeble smile of a crazy man, I'd believe it.

I didn't think about Meryl Streep or Jack Nicholson or Sean Penn anymore.

I didn't think about the plot points we'd spent so long identifying.

I thought only about sentences, sentences that for some reason meant something, sentences that fit together one after the other like a puzzle I already knew, knew by heart, and they meant something.

I don't think farmers have ever fallen victim to that kind of frenzy.

Though there must be farmers who imagine entire movies while they harvest vegetables and fruit.

Harvest movies.

Plant a screenplay in a square meter of fertile earth, water it, and after a few days harvest a movie that's brilliantly directed and acted and lit and edited.

The quality depends on the type of fertilizer you use when you plant the screenplay.

Hollywood is Monsanto: thousands of acres where they sow and harvest their thousands of Roundup movies.

The screenplay I wrote that Sunday afternoon/evening and early Monday morning is organic.

No, even better: that screenplay was planted without chemicals, organic or otherwise, harvested solely through the virtue of Mother

Nature, a Mother Nature who had the gall . . . no, the *wisdom* to create me, birth me, to bring me into the world, a man scrupulously designed to live in a basement, to accept imprisonment in exchange for the most sublime art, in exchange for change.

How many screenplays did Aristotle write?

How many screenplays did Robert McKee write?

How many screenplays did Syd Field write?

Sometimes I peered at what I'd written and I nodded, yes yes yes, and I went on writing, the scenes leaping from my mind like the desperate artists who jumped the Berlin Wall during the Cold War.

The writer's block was a wall.

An invented wall.

A wall that existed, but wasn't real.

Going into Monday I had forty-nine pages written.

Don't even think about stopping and reading them, I told myself. There is no Monday. There was no Sunday, there is no Monday. Santiago isn't going to come down and bother me, never again, because he said Monday and Monday isn't coming.

It was already Monday, I saw out of the corner of my eye: twelve-oh-seven.

One of the characters asks the time and the other replies:

Seven past twelve.

Nothing more insignificant than for one character to ask another the time.

Unless it's an action movie and the bomb is about to explode.

My bomb was about to explode.

Tick tock, tick tock, tick tock, tick tock, tick tock.

Apparently, my bomb was the old-fashioned kind.

My fingers tried to grasp the essential, they swept aside all that was extraneous with one of those little archaeological brushes.

Two hands, fifteen fingers.

I didn't use my thumbs or little fingers.

Nine fingers.

I don't know who the extra three fingers belonged to.

Here on the bus I'm using a pen I borrowed from the woman next to me.

She asked me why I was going to Buenos Aires.

I told her I live in Buenos Aires, that I'd gone to San Martín de los Andes on vacation, a vacation that was originally meant to last two weeks and wound up lasting a lot longer.

Yes, she said, San Martín is very nice. Makes you want to stick around, doesn't it?

The pen is an extension of my right hand that acts as a finger tracing words I can barely read, not because I get dizzy reading them (although I do get dizzy), but because my handwriting is pathetic, as if I were using the Arabic alphabet to write in Spanish.

*   *   *

Most likely, there is no Dr. Miranda; Santiago must have invented him to pacify me, soothe me.

Good thing I didn't have molar pain.

If I'd had a toothache, Santiago would have yanked out my molar with pliers, the way he imagined doing to himself when he got to the United States, so the Writers Guild people would have to spend some of his insurance money on him.

I don't know who removed my gallstones.

I don't know how, or when, or where.

I only know that on that Monday morning, after Santiago read the screenplay I'd finished minutes before, he looked at me with an indecipherable expression (I still don't know what that look meant), and then he asked me if I was all right.

I thought he was going to start in on a lecture, give me a whole spiel, explain to me why the screenplay he'd just read didn't work, but no, he left the laptop on the floor and came over to the mattress, and in that moment, because of how he was looking at me, I realized that I had both hands on the right side of my abdomen, that I was pressing on my gallbladder (I still didn't know it was my gallbladder), and I also realized (understood) that if I stopped pressing on the right side of my abdomen, the pain was going to take over everything, or I felt that if I took my hands from the right side of my abdomen, the pain was going to kill me.

I don't remember clearly what happened next.

Santiago's face strangely close to mine, one of his hands on my forehead.

Norma with a glass of water, or what I assumed was water.

I remember what I felt when I drank it: water that was cold when it touched my lips, but boiling as it went down my throat.

I asked Norma if it was mineral water.

She didn't answer.

They didn't talk to me.

They talked to each other, among themselves.

Was there someone else?

Malone Dies goes to the island with me.

Ulysses is an overly written book.

Joyce writes fully convinced that he knows what it is to be Jewish, what it is to be Irish, what it is to be a woman.

Beckett writes convinced that he doesn't know anything; he writes to try to find something out, aware that he will never know it fully.

Beckett writes the only way that's worthwhile.

Erudition is overvalued; it's much harder to write when you don't know anything.

We should force people who've never read a book to write
one paragraph a hundred and fifty pages long in the first person,
force them at gunpoint, millions of *Malone Dieses*, and then set
fire to them—to the paragraphs, not the people, and then to the
people, too.

People who think they're writers are the ones who write the worst.

Writing is not a profession, it's the best way to waste a life.

Piles of notebooks full of wasted time.

Rolls and rolls of film full of wasted time.

The film world (which is not a world) is overflowing with people
who think they know what they're doing.

Film professionals, they're called.

Thousands of writers convinced they know how to write.

Aristotle's dumb kids.

Santiago and Norma were talking to Aristotle in the basement,
deciding what to do with me, when the only thing I wanted was to
know what Santiago had thought of the screenplay.

I asked him, but the words wouldn't leave my mouth.

*   *   *

Chekhov's paternal grandfather was the slave of a certain Chertkov,
and he saved up the money to buy his freedom, his own and his wife's
and that of their three sons; and Count Chertkov generously also
granted him the freedom of his daughter (Chekhov's grandfather's
daughter), Aleksandra.

I don't know why I remember that anecdote.

The son of a bitch bought his freedom and his wife's and his
sons', but not his only daughter's?

Couldn't he have saved a little more?

We forget the cruelty people used to live with.

I'm not saying there isn't cruelty now, there's more than enough cruelty all around us, but back then . . .

Institutionalized cruelty.

These days, people get offended over any old bullshit.

People—that is: the audience.

It's exhausting to write with the fear of offending people.

Impossible to write well without offending people.

Scarface with a black actor would have been a racist movie.

Are you saying that black people are all drug traffickers and murderers?

Taxi Driver with a Japanese man.

American Psycho with a Latino.

Latin Psycho.

Better not to write.

If you don't write, you don't offend anyone.

In *Malone Dies*, Beckett can't offend anyone because he doesn't write.

Ulysses was censored for years, in the United States as well as in England and Ireland, because the censors could tell it had been written.

I didn't write the screenplay that was supposed to change the course of film history, I ejaculated it, and I couldn't know what Santiago thought of my screenplay because the pain kept me from understanding what he was saying to me.

I fainted.

I don't know if I fainted from the pain, or because they'd put something in the water.

I woke up on the mattress in the basement, just like any other morning of those five-plus years, free of pain, or with a very slight pain that was different from the previous pain, and I lifted my shirt and found the bandage covering my stomach.

It was hard to sit up.

Why did I never ask for a chair?

Five years at floor level.

Sometimes I sat on the minifridge, or on the bag of dirty clothes.

I waited for Santiago to come downstairs.

He didn't come.

He'd taken the laptop.

I waited for Norma to come downstairs.

The sun's brightness in the rectangle told me it was already almost noon.

No sign of my coffee, or the little dish of fruit.

I was hungry and thirsty.

I crawled slowly to the minifridge and opened it: empty.

This is it, I thought, they're letting me die.

Then I asked myself: If they're going to let me die, then why'd they remove whatever was lighting a bonfire in the right side of my abdomen?

I waited several hours.

Night fell.

I don't know if it was night, but the rectangle went dark.

I thought about playing a couple Beatles songs on the ukelele, but when I picked it up, the desire left me.

The absence of the laptop loomed larger every minute; it was like losing your best friend in an accident, like losing the world.

I was still in the world, in the basement that was my world, but at the same time, I was missing my world.

I heard footsteps on the stairs.

I had never gone up or down those stairs.

I'd been carried up or down (or at least once down, after that dinner with Santiago when we talked about everything), but I had never set foot on the steps themselves.

I didn't know they were cement until I climbed them last night.

Though I always imagined they were cement.

What other material could they have been?

Wood?

A cement basement with wooden stairs?

Norma came down with dinner: broth with angel hair pasta, water, two slices of white sandwich bread, and two pills.

I asked her what the pills were.

She didn't answer me.

She motioned for me to take them.

Where's Santiago? I asked. I need to talk to him.

Norma held out her right hand with the palm down, and then she raised it in a diagonal line, a gesture that tends to mean "plane taking off."

Impossible, I said. To the United States?

No answer.

Where's my laptop?

No answer.

Did he leave it upstairs?

No answer.

Could you see if he left it upstairs?

No answer.

I need my laptop. Tell Santiago I need it.

She didn't say anything.

She opened the valve oxygen tank and stood there for a while, looking at me, in silence, the revolver tucked into her apron pocket.

I'm sorry, Norma, I told her. I want to apologize for . . . the other day. I don't know what came over me.

She stood there, looking at me, in silence.

The truth is, I'd like for us to talk, I told her. Have a conversation, learn about your family in Mexico.

Stood there, looking at me, in silence.

How long has it been since you've seen them?

Stood there, looking at me, in silence.

Norma is synonymous with "silence."

Most of the bus passengers travel in Norma.

Norma is golden.

Norma speaks louder than words.

The word is time and Norma, eternity.

Slave to the word and master of Norma.

Better to be king of Norma than a slave to your words.

Keep Norma, Betances, or I'll send you to the principal's office!

Stood there, looking at me, in Norma.

She turned off the oxygen tank and left.

*   *   *

I've just gone to the bathroom, a tiny closet with a preschool-sized toilet and a broken sink.

While I pissed, I leaned my head against the uncurved wall of the bus.

Would I have preferred for it to be curved?

Wait for some turbulence to . . . ?

I hope my old man was able to put away his penis and zip up his pants before he died of a broken neck.

The girl isn't a girl, she's a boy around eighteen years old wearing a San Lorenzo shirt and shorts.

Mozart managed to make it really far.

Much farther than Fellini.

Much farther than Shakespeare.

A whole lot farther than Joyce.

I went an entire month with no news from Santiago.

Norma came down as usual, in silence, without my laptop.

I had nothing to do besides play the ukelele, masturbate, and sleep.

One morning she came down with the cup of coffee and the little dish of fruit, left them beside the mattress (I still hadn't emerged from the sheets and blanket), and gestured for me to pull the covers back, and I pulled the covers back, and then she gestured for me to take my shirt off, and I took it off, and then with a third gesture she asked me to remove the bandage, and I removed it, and for the first time I saw my scar, a five-centimeter stripe to the right of my stomach that had been sewn without thread (*glued*, not *sewn*).

Who did this to me? I asked.

No answer.

Who fixed my pain?

No answer.

I still didn't know what had caused the pain.

I didn't know what they had done to me, and I couldn't imagine, either, because I didn't know what had caused the pain.

Could you bring me down some books? I asked.

No answer.

Any book, I said. Whatever you find up there. I know Santiago has books upstairs. A lot. Choose whichever one you want. How about one book a week. What do you say?

No answer.

She took the bandage with her and closed the door.

I would have paid a fortune (if I'd had a fortune to pay) for a copy of the screenplay I'd written in the frenzy of that Sunday afternoon/evening and early Monday morning.

Though if I had a fortune to pay, and if I'd paid that fortune in exchange for the screenplay I'd written that Sunday afternoon/evening and early Monday morning, I would have started to read it with an unbearable fear.

I don't know what I wrote.

I don't know if what I wrote was good.

I guess it was, because Santiago took it away without a word.

I guess it wasn't, because Santiago took it away without a word, and he hired another screenwriter, and he left me to die in the basement.

No, I know full well that Santiago didn't hire another screenwriter, or leave me to die in the basement.

He left me *alive* in the basement, in the prison of the basement, as alive as could be, and then he came back with his revolver.

*   *   *

A bossa nova version of "I Wanna Be Sedated" is playing over the bus speakers.

How much longer until we're there?

Eleven and a half hours, according to the woman sitting next to me.

She asked me what I was writing.

Notes, I told her.

Notes? What kind?

Notes for a book I'm going to write when I get to Buenos Aires.

(I'm not going to write a book when I get to Buenos Aires.)

A novel? she asked.

Yes.

What's it about?

A ski instructor who teaches at Chapelco and solves crimes in his free time.

I don't think there are many crimes to solve in San Martín, she said.

There are always crimes to solve, I told her, everywhere, all the time.

The woman looked at me the way Santiago did when I said something he considered an exaggeration; the woman's eyes don't look anything like Santiago's, but the look was the same.

The copilot or codriver came through handing out Jorgito *alfajores*, chocolate or *dulce de leche* (you had to choose one; I chose chocolate), and a kind of lemonade, or mineral water with artificial lemon flavor, Villa del Sur brand.

The months I spent in the basement sans laptop or notebook or books turned me into a more than passable ukelele player.

Mostly, I freestyled chords, but I also learned complicated songs, like "While My Guitar Gently Weeps," or "Jugo de lúcuma," which I managed to play from memory.

I should have taken the ukelele.

An instrument made entirely from carbon fiber must be worth a fortune.

As soon as I save some money I'll buy one, a cheap wooden one.

Though it's going to be hard to get used to the sound of a cheap wooden ukelele after months of going to town on a carbon fiber one.

I touch the right side of my abdomen and don't feel a thing.

Maybe they took everything out, maybe they removed the right side of my stomach, whatever organs are there on the right side.

The truth is that this semi-sleeper seat isn't so bad.

I'd be capable of living in this seat for entire years, so long as I could stand up for a while and walk down the aisle, at least once every ten hours, when I go to the bathroom, and also so long as I had my laptop, and a plug for my laptop, and some higher-quality earphones than these Califone ones, and a copilot or codriver who brings me chocolate *alfajores* and mineral water every three or four hours.

I feel sorry for people who try to encapsulate the whole world.

Santiago tried to encapsulate the whole world.

Did I try to encapsulate the whole world with my screenplays?

No, because my screenplays aren't mine.

I accepted that years ago, and went on writing them.

I'm an admirable person.

Pathetic.

Pathetically admirable.

I never imagined that the screenplay about the boy who throws his family into a well could encapsulate the whole world; I wrote it because I wanted to write it, because I liked to sit and write, write anything, not because I thought that absurd story would make the world kneel down before me.

The world doesn't kneel before anyone anymore.

Joyce tried to encapsulate the whole world; with what remained of his eyes he sought to make the whole world kneel at his feet, and he managed it, at least for a while.

Today, few people kneel at the feet of *Ulysses*—not enough even to fill the Monumental stadium in Buenos Aires.

Beckett didn't try to encapsulate any world.

When he won the Nobel Prize, he set out for Africa, hid away in a village where there'd recently been a flood, and said that because of the flood he couldn't attend the ceremony.

He invented a flood.

Joyce would have landed in Sweden in a gilded hot-air balloon, shouting at the top of his lungs: *I'm the greatest thing that's happened to literature since Homer!*

*   *   *

What will I do if I get home and my old lady doesn't live there anymore?

I'll ask the doorman where she is.

And if the doorman doesn't know?

I'll ask Silvia, the neighbor in 9D, who came down once a week to ask my old lady to let her use our computer to see if her niece, the only member of her family she loved, had sent her an email.

And if Silvia doesn't know?

I'll call Uncle Manuel, my old lady's brother, who lives in Campana.

Manuel has to know if my old lady moved, or if she's no longer capable of moving.

What will I do if my old lady is dead?

I'll look for Lisandro.

And if Lisandro is dead?

It wouldn't surprise me if Santiago had them killed.

Yes, it would surprise me; Santiago wasn't a murderer, he was an artist.

A desperate artist.

One of those artists who constantly seek to outdo themselves, and who live in constant anxiety, and who are capable of going to the utmost extremes so they can reach the greatest artistic heights.

I'm pretty sure that when I think about my mother I scrunch up my face, like I'm trying to bring my eyes and mouth closer to my nose; after I think about my old lady for a while, the middle of my face feels hot.

Santiago laughed twice while reading the screenplay.

Usually, when he read scenes in front of me and I saw him smile, or laugh, or guffaw, I'd ask him: What? And he'd reply: this or that line of dialogue or action.

But that Monday morning I kept quiet; during the hour it took Santiago to read the screenplay (a hundred and thirty-nine pages), neither of us let out a single sound except his two laughs and a dumb, painful cough that forced me to go to the bathroom and gargle.

Before he started on the first act, Santiago took out one of his imported chocolates (a Godiva with four big squares filled with pistachio cream) and stuffed the whole thing in his mouth, not square by square but all at once, and he chewed slowly as he read.

In three months, I perfected a set of twenty-five songs on the ukelele.

One morning I played it for Norma.

I didn't play the whole set, because when I was going into the fifth song, "The Fool on the Hill," Norma (who had started to clean the bathroom) flushed the toilet several times in a row and interrupted my inspiration.

I still don't know how I managed to play twenty-five songs from memory.

I'm capable of remembering each and every Beatles song along with chords, arrangements, and melodies, but not one complete scene of that screenplay that was supposed to change the course of world cinema history.

A screenplay that followed the incomplete, deleted screenplay step by step, and at the same time was completely new; it was like someone reproducing a painting from memory while simultaneously being swept along by inspiration.

I accepted each and every spark that occurred to me, inserting it into the scene right as it appeared.

Aaron Sorkin would have shit himself laughing.

But really, what great script did Aaron Sorkin ever write?

What Sorkin film will they study for decades to come in film schools around the world?

I should have used some of the thousands of hours in the basement to learn a language.

English, maybe—I could translate my own screenplays.

I could translate the crossed-out notebook.

I should have asked Norma to . . .

Waited for her to come down and begged her to . . .

If Norma hadn't been so hopelessly stubborn, she'd have let me . . .

Norma wasn't stubborn; I don't know what she was—what she is.

There was something in me she didn't like.

Something that Santiago had shown her, or that she herself had seen in me and that she detested.

My old man also saw that thing in me.

He never said anything about it, but I know he saw it, because of the way he looked at me, or rather the way he avoided looking at me.

A spiritual apathy.

An innate condition that dulled my world.

An anemia of the soul, an autumnal spring fever, which didn't keep me from moving about naturally, no, there were even days when I woke up feeling healthy and energetic and wanting to do things, but those things, even if they were fun or important or unexpected, lacked sparkle, as if someone had polished them too many times.

My old lady never noticed that lack in me.

At least, I don't think she did.

My old man seemed to want to help me (though I didn't feel the need for help, or feel it now), but he never made up his mind to do it.

Norma had perceived that bit of soul I was missing (that is, she perceived the vacant space), and she detested me for it.

I never thought she would help me.

I couldn't help thinking about Norma while I was writing the character Meryl Streep would play.

Every time she appeared, Norma appeared.

I killed her off in the end.

If I remember correctly, and it's likely that I don't (I can't wait to lie down in bed with my old lady to watch the pirated copy of that movie I wrote and Santiago directed and that was supposed to change the course of world cinema history), I had her jump from her building's balcony and hit the pavement face-first.

*　　*　　*

I guess I should have called my old lady.

Why *didn't* I call her?

Why don't I ask any one of the other passengers if I can borrow their cell phone, and call her?

I don't remember the number.

Yes, I remember it.

No, I never knew the number of my old lady's cell, I had it stored on mine.

No one memorizes numbers anymore.

I remember one number, but I don't remember who it belongs to.

I could ask to borrow a phone and dial that number.

What did Santiago do with my phone?

Did he turn it off?

Did he sit in the comfortable armchair in his study with its view of trees and sky and wait for people to call me?

How many times did my old lady call?

And Lisandro?

How much does Patricia know about what happened?

Does Patricia still exist?

Santiago never uttered her name in the basement.

We talked briefly about Patricia during that dinner when we talked about everything, but after that he never mentioned her again.

Santiago never brought his cell phone down to the basement.

Every once in a while, rarely, Norma came down with the home phone and indicated with a gesture: you have a call.

One morning during my second month in the basement, I asked Santiago if Norma was mute.

No, he said. Why?

She doesn't talk to me, I told him.

He looked at me the way he did when I made him talk about something he didn't want to talk about.

I ask her questions and she doesn't answer, I told him. Not a peep. Like I don't exist.

That's Norma's business, Pablo. Why do you want to talk to her anyway? Leave her alone. She's got enough work keeping this place clean and habitable. Plus, she cooks like the gods.

Yeah, the gods of hell.

He didn't laugh.

I wonder if Santiago and Norma . . .

Sometimes I caught them exchanging looks.

Once, they caught me catching them exchanging a look.

They were hiding something.

A relationship that went beyond *master of the house* and *housekeeper*.

I asked the woman sitting next to me if she had a cell phone, and she told me she did but it didn't have much battery left.

That was it.

That's all I'm going to do about the only phone number I can remember.

Once, when we were working on the first screenplay, I asked Santiago to let me call my old lady and tell her I was okay, and apologize, to tell her I had to leave, take some time for myself, decide what to do with my life, but I'm okay, Ma, don't worry, I'll call you when I'm coming back.

He said no.

You'll only worry her more, he said. She won't believe you, and you'll leave her triply worried. Do you know how to lie, Pablo? Do you know how to act?

He made me read one of our scenes, act it out, and when I finished he looked at me the way he did when I'd said something funny but he didn't want to show me he'd found it funny, and then he burst out laughing, and he said no again, this time shaking his head, he said it several times, no, no no no no no no, and he started to talk about something else.

Acting is hard.

Acting is practically impossible.

I have enormous admiration for actors.

They don't even need to be great for me to admire them.

Once, on the set of the first and only screenplay I ever sold, in Buenos Aires, the director's assistant saw me standing there doing nothing, drinking my fourth coffee (I'd discovered that the best thing about film sets is the catering service, with its variety of drinks and teas and sandwiches and sweets), and he informed me that the camera to my right was going to film the street, a wide-angle shot of the street, of people walking, extras simulating people walking, and he needed someone to pass five or six times in front of the camera, one meter from the camera, to cast shadows, shadows of people walking, from one side to another, and I told him I wasn't an actor, I didn't know how to act, and he told me not to worry, no one was going to see me, I was only going to be a shadow, several shadows, and then I agreed, I told him "No problem," and he grabbed me forcefully by the arm and set me to one side of the camera and told me to wait, he'd tell me when to cross in front of the lens, and I said "Okay," and while I was waiting I started to get more and more nervous, I didn't understand why I was so nervous, and someone shouted "Action," and I stood stiff and looked at the assistant until he signaled to me with his right hand, and I crossed in front of the camera trying to walk as naturally as possible, but it was impossible to walk naturally, my whole body was one long muscle, no limbs, no joints, a piece of meat that could only move slowly, very slowly, and I turned and crossed again, my body stiffer and stiffer, and I crossed again, until someone shouted "Cut" and the assistant came over with a smile and asked me, "Didn't anyone ever teach you how to walk?" and he went walking calmly away, and there I stood, still stiff, holding my coffee, now almost cold, wondering why, if no one could see me, if I was nothing but a shadow, I had suffered such paralysis, why I was so nervous, and the only explanation was that I wasn't an actor, I'm not an actor, I don't know how to act, and it had become very clear to me that acting is hard, very hard, practically impossible.

No one went to see that movie; it played for a week at the Gaumont, and that was that.

The trees scattered across the countryside are the very definition of mediocrity.

Low quality, almost bad.

Lacking value or interest.

Most screenwriters are like those trees, we're thought to lack value and interest.

A screenwriter on the set of his own movie is like one of those useless trees.

Worse than those useless trees, because we're not even good for building a bird's nest or beehive in our armpits, or for a kid to attach a car tire with two ropes to one of our arms and make a swing.

*   *   *

Am I going to miss the silence of the basement?

Am I going to miss the smell of the basement—that is, my smell and the smell of my farts?

Am I going to miss Norma?

Am I going to wake up in the morning next to my mother and expect Norma to come in with breakfast?

Am I going to need to ask my old lady to make me a cup of coffee every morning (not Dolca, but filtered coffee, nice and black with a slight hint of tobacco), and to cut different fruits into little cubes and arrange them on a dessert plate?

How easy it is to write questions.

But for some reason, just now, it's important to array them on the un-crossed-out pages of this notebook.

How many do I have left?

I should have bought another notebook at the minimart, or at least one of those flimsy little notepads people use for shopping lists.

The fingernail against the window plays the chorus from "Tirá para arriba."

Ta ta, ta ta ta ta ta ta, ta ta.

Ta is not the right monosyllable to identify the sound of a fingernail against a window.

The Gilda album has started to play again over the bus speakers.

I hold the pen too tightly; after writing by hand a while, I feel it cramping up and I stop to stretch it, and then I pick up the pen and keep writing.

It's as if I don't trust my hand: I use it to hold the pen and write, but at the same time I'm afraid it's going to let go of its own accord, or drive the pen into my eye.

Five hours until we reach the Capital.

The highway occasionally turns into a street with stoplights, traffic, and people waiting to cross.

I smell burnt coffee.

A few minutes later they're serving it to us in Styrofoam cups, along with a paper napkin wrapped around a little packet of sugar, another of powdered milk, and a plastic stick to stir.

Hopefully Dolca instant coffee still exists.

Something so essential for life can't cease to exist just like that.

*　　*　　*

One recommendable exercise is to retype the screenplay entirely.

When you finish the first draft—what Philip Roth called "the vomited draft"—let it rest for a few days, then read it, correct it, mark what doesn't work (if you know someone who is a good reader, and honest, who isn't afraid of hurting your feelings, give it to them to read), collect notes, take them into consideration, then attack the second draft, let it rest, read it, correct it while you read, let it rest, and then retype it completely, print it out, and set it up next to the laptop or PC or typewriter and repeat it, word for word, rewriting the phrases that don't work.

Aaron Sorkin, one of Hollywood's greatest screenplay diagrammers, told Santiago at a dinner for the Writers Guild of America that at the end of writing, after the third or fourth draft, he rewrites the whole thing from memory: he opens a blank file and retypes the screenplay without looking at the previous draft even out of the corner of his eye.

Life is like a box of chocolates, said Forrest Gump—or Eric Roth, *Forrest Gump*'s screenwriter and another Hollywood diagrammer—but he forgot to add that the chocolates are almost always hollow, filled with poisonous air.

How much does a ticket to Los Angeles cost?

I'll buy two, first class.

Let the Writers Guild of America pay for them.

*   *   *

We no longer go up or down; only very rarely do we turn right or left.

Several hours ago the copilot or codriver took over for the pilot or driver, and the pilot or driver moved aside, immediately becoming the copilot or codriver.

It doesn't seem like a bad job: life on the highway.

A basement on wheels.

Not to belong anywhere, to be from everywhere and nowhere.

Although I wouldn't like to be in charge of so many people.

Too many hours of responsibility.

Plus, I never learned to drive.

My old man tried to teach me, but I was easily distracted; I got bored, and boredom while driving is a cause of death; I had trouble figuring out speed; I slammed on the brakes, or braked a little too late; I forgot to slow down before turning; I sped up when the thing to do was ease off the accelerator.

My old man deserved a medal for his patience.

My old lady doesn't drive, either.

When my old man died, we sold the car and used some of the money to buy two very expensive Italian bicycles that we only used on Sunday mornings on the bicycle path in the Palermo parks, until three kids in Milton Nascimento T-shirts (all three wore the same shirt) told us to stop and hand over the bikes, without pulling any weapons at us, and my old lady and I did just that, we dropped the bikes on the ground and took off running.

Later, when we got home, my old lady asked me what I wanted for lunch, and I told her I wasn't hungry, but she insisted that we had to eat something, and she started to cook some scrambled eggs, which, after I swallowed them, left a slightly metallic taste on the back of my tongue.

The pilot or driver, who a while ago was the copilot or codriver, drives much more roughly than the other pilot or driver, who is now resting in the hollow above the first row of seats, enjoying one of his privileges as copilot or codriver.

The signs along the highway name places I didn't know existed and that after a few minutes I'll forget.

I tried to sleep.

I couldn't.

With my eyes closed, I counted two hundred twenty-five clicks.

Buenos Aires is close, I can feel it.

When I say "Buenos Aires," I say "the Capital."

All *porteños* say "the Capital" when they say "Buenos Aires."

Santiago slept three hours a day.

Sometimes a thirty-minute nap after lunch.

He loved the number three.

Our screenplays always had to have ninety-three, or a hundred and three, or a hundred and thirty, or a hundred twenty-three pages.

He told me he hadn't had another child because he didn't want to break the three.

The screenplay I finished a year ago, the one that was supposed to change the course of world cinema history, had a hundred and thirty-nine pages.

One three.

A nine, which is made of three threes.

Three hours left.

I'm not positive, but let's say there are three left.

How am I going to get from Retiro to Belgrano?

In what?

I don't have a single peso in cash.

Can you pay taxis with a card the way Santiago said you can in the United States?

I'll sneak into the subway.

If they catch me, I'll say I can pay the fine with a card, and I'll ask them to sell me a ticket while they're at it.

It took Santiago nearly two years to come back; nearly two years passed between my loss of consciousness and his reappearance in the basement.

I don't know how much of those nearly two years he spent on preproduction, how much on production, how much on postproduction, how much on promotion.

Nearly two years I spent clutching the ukelele like it was the only tree trunk floating in the middle of a savage sea.

How could I be so thoughtless as to leave it in the basement?

Nearly two years I practically didn't utter a word that wasn't a Beatles or Spinetta lyric.

Santiago agreed that Spinetta is the Argentine musician who reached the greatest heights, even greater than Piazzolla and Ginastera, much greater than Atahualpa Yupanqui.

Could there be some musician version of Santiago who hides an anonymous composer in a basement full of instruments?

Santiago used to tell me how much he liked jazz, but I know deep down he hated it.

I was always afraid of jazz.

I tried to become a Pat Metheny addict like so many of my teachers and classmates at the Buenos Aires School of Music, but ultimately I had to admit (to myself) that Metheny was too good for me.

I was lucky to be born in an age when it isn't necessary to be a genius, or even incredibly talented, to leave a mark on the world.

Quantity doesn't ensure quality.

Maybe one of my greatest limitations as a writer of both literature and screenplays was the constant need for a mentor, a guide, a writer whose footsteps I could follow, to whom I could compare everything I did and everything everyone else did.

I could never write anything without the presence of—

Presence of, no; *veneration of*: without venerating.

Several times over the course of my life as a writer I tried to write without reading, without venerating, and I put all my books into a cardboard box my old lady used to store Disney masks in, and I hid it at the back of the storage room among the suitcases with my old man's belongings that my old lady hadn't been able to give away yet, and I forced myself to live like that for several days, without books, with only my notebooks and the PC, and at first I managed to make progress in whatever it was I was writing, but then, after a few days, an uncomfortable anxiety rose up from my stomach every time I sat down to write, and then the writer's block appeared, like an empty room with the walls stained from damp, and the room would replace my mind little by little, and the need to read other people would eat away at me, push me toward meaninglessness, and writing was suddenly a stupid act, an impossible and unnecessary act, and then I'd run to the storage room and get the box and put the books back where they belonged.

Writing is reading.

I spend most of my writing time reading.

At least, that's how it was until my last year in the basement.

As I was writing the first two screenplays for Santiago, I read widely.

Then, going into the fifth year in the basement, something changed.

Writing scenes started to be like pulling teeth.

Writing scenes started to, as we say in Argentina, cost me a Peru.

But how much does Peru cost?

I don't think Peru is very expensive.

It cost me a Vatican.

Writing became a job, an utterly professional profession.

My constant reading slowed down because writing demanded more and more effort, more and more concentration.

Whenever I was reading other people I was thinking about how I should be writing, and the words would pass by without meaning.

I'd read the same page three times, four times, the same paragraph, the same line.

I'm going to buy a kilo of Freddo *dulce de leche* chocolate chip gelato.

* * *

The bus windows don't open.

The only air comes from the air conditioner.

I emerged from an airless basement just so that a few hours later I could lock myself in an airless bus.

Santiago appeared in the basement with no advance warning, his expression clenched, as if he had a canary in his mouth and didn't want to let it out.

I threw the covers off and sat up on the mattress.

There was no cup of coffee.

No little dish of fruit.

No laptop.

No Golden Globe.

No Oscar.

The butt of the revolver peeked out at his right hip.

Santiago looked the basement over as if it were his childhood home and he was returning for the first time in fifty years.

His eyes fell on the ukelele:

Gustavo left me twenty messages asking for it back. (Pause.) You broke a string.

I nodded.

How long ago?

A couple months. I had to learn to play with three. At first I thought it wasn't going to work, but—

It's a good number, three.

I nodded.

Norma told me you spent all your time playing, he said.

I nodded.

Joyce would have mocked Santiago in *Ulysses* if Santiago had lived in Dublin in 1904.

He sat on the minifridge.

And? I asked.

And what?

Did we do it?

Do what?

Change world cinema history.

When?

What do you mean, when?

World cinema history is the Atacama Desert, Pablo. How do you change a desert?

I don't understand.

Of course you don't understand, there's nothing to understand.

How was Los Angeles?

Good.

What does "good" mean?

Nice town. Pleasant weather. Never rains.

Talk to me about the movie.

What movie?

Ours.

A smile sliced his face from ear to ear.

Ninety-seven million, he said. Over fifty on publicity. They figure we're not even going to get a quarter of it back. The head of Universal shook my hand and said: This is as far as we go. (Pause.) I made a huge mistake, Pablo.

What happened?

I listened to you. I never should . . . The best first draft I've read in my life. The words got embedded behind my eyes in perfect images. A miracle, Pablo. A fucking miracle. How could you rewrite it all in two weeks?

One night.

You're lying.

I rewrote it in one afternoon/evening and early morning. I spent I don't know how many days with writer's block, until on Sunday at—

Doesn't matter. A miracle. I felt like crying, and hugging you, but in your face there was a . . . I don't know . . . repressed panic, something much more urgent than my desire to cry and hug you.

Do you have a copy?

No.

I'd like to see it.

He stood up, walked to the bathroom, turned on the faucet— I heard water hitting the sink for several seconds—then he turned the water off and came out of the bathroom.

We didn't get into Cannes, he said. They accepted it in Un Certain Regard, which is the same thing as not getting into Cannes. Two days before the premiere I called Thierry Frémaux and told him I wasn't going. I apologized and said I'd had pneumonia and couldn't finish postproduction. He didn't believe me. I could tell from his voice that he didn't believe me. I decided it was better not to premiere at festivals. If it's not the official Cannes competition, there's nothing left in Europe. We premiered in L.A. in September.

An all-out gala, the crème de la crème of Hollywood. At Grauman's Chinese Theater. Catering by David Chang. John Scofield played at the cocktail party after the screening. But I didn't go to the cock-tail party. I said I had a headache. As I was leaving the theater, the whispering made my blood run cold. I had to wait months after the movie was ready because the people at Universal decided to premiere near the end of the year. They said it would help with nominations. The movie would still be fresh when the old folks in the Academy started voting.

You could have come here during those months, visited me, brought me the laptop, some books. You don't know how hard it was to endure almost two years with nothing but my ukelele.

It's not your ukulele.

In a way it is.

No.

Ask him. Ask him if he wants to go back to Gustavo or stay with me.

It doesn't matter, Pablo, the ukulele is going back to Gustavo.

Ask him.

He came over to me and put a hand on my shoulder.

He didn't usually come so close to me.

I remember only two hugs: the first one years ago, after he aimed the revolver at me and spun the chamber and pulled the trigger, and the second time the night he came down drunk with the Oscar for Best Foreign Language Film.

He tended to keep his distance, as if after all these years he still didn't have full confidence in me.

He squeezed my shoulder with his non-writer fingers, and then he brought his face close to mine, so close I thought he was going to kiss me on the mouth, but no, he sniffed my beard, coughed, and asked me how long it had been since I showered.

Months, I told him.

How many months?

I don't remember.

You smell like a bum from Constitución.

I doubt that Santiago has ever been in Constitución, much less gotten close enough to a bum to smell him.

He moved away toward the rectangle of light and leaned his head against the cement, his back to me.

I told him Norma had treated me very badly.

I ask her for books and she doesn't bring them, I said. I ask her for a piece of paper to write on and—

She told me about the assault, he said.

What assault?

She said you tried to . . . You know what? I understand, Pablo. I don't blame you.

I told him:

I thought I was going to die of boredom. I sank into the depths of boredom, Santiago. The days lasted weeks, and, toward the end, months. Every time I went to bed, whatever time it was, I counted the number of days that day had lasted. Ninety-five was the record. One day that lasted ninety-five days.

Ninety has thirty threes, he said.

The goat smell agreed to be my best friend. My *second*-best friend, because my best friend is Uke.

You don't have the slightest fucking idea, do you?

About what?

About what you wrote.

What did I write?

The screenplay. The rewrite. Was it really one night?

Afternoon/evening and early morning.

Incredible. An extraordinary leap. Did you take anything?

No.

The fasting. Maybe that was it. A Buddhist draft. (Pause.) Doctor Miranda took care of everything. Gallstones. Excesses of mediocrity that gradually built up there, letting the genius spill out over the pages, nothing but genius, everything else piled up in your gallbladder. The doctor told me he'd never seen such large stones.

What did they give me?

The doctor doesn't exist anymore, Pablo. He had an accident on the highway driving to Chos Malal. It's a shame. Good guy, that doctor.

If someone could recover the terabytes of thoughts that went through my mind (flashes of stupidity and fear and desperation) and download them to an external hard drive with a large storage capacity . . .

A basemented Molly Bloom.

The farce of an interior monologue.

Artificial exercise of thought.

Plagiarized letters from Nora, Joyce's hotel maid.

More real than . . .

Much more real than the pile of thoughts I've been accumulating and losing in these nearly two years of tedium.

Monday afternoon I read it again, said Santiago, and it seemed even better. I only made a couple of notes that I figured the translator could correct. And I figured right. That same Monday night I left for New York. On Tuesday I had dinner with the translator at a very good restaurant in the East Village, Saxon and Parole, or Saxon plus Parole, and I promised to double her fee if she could translate the screenplay in five days. She did an admirable job. Since I can't trust my English, I gave it to my manager and my agents to read, and all three called me after a few hours to congratulate me and tell me it was one of the best screenplays they'd read in a long time. I read it again that night, and the next morning I called the translator to ask her for some final corrections, and she didn't take long to send it to me again, corrected, and, obsessive as I am, I read it again, and when I finished, I sent it to the actors. The replies from Jack and Meryl and Sean were immediate and incredibly positive. Jack proposed we offer the role of Lisa to Jennifer Lawrence. My agents got in touch with hers, and, after confirming she was free during the months I planned to film, we sent her the screenplay. Jennifer called me the next morning to say she was definitely in, and that it was by far one of the most exciting reads she'd had since she started working in Hollywood. So much positivity ended up convincing me, Pablo. I almost called you to . . . (Pause.) I never brought you the lesson book for the ukulele.

No, you never did.

I have it upstairs. How did you manage to learn so many songs without . . . ?

All the time in the world, I said. And even though my hands leave plenty to be desired, my ear is more than respectable. At the music school my ear was one of the best, but my hands were among the worst hands.

A miracle, Pablo. The new *Smultronstället*.

Say what?

Bergman. *Wild Strawberries*. *Fresas salvajes*. *Frutillas salvajes*. *Cuando huye el día*. A script that should be published in book form. One hundred thirty-nine pages. I let the financiers know I was going to need another twenty-seven million. They didn't object. Happy with the script. Exultant. I thought about telling them you had written it. No, can you imagine what a mess it would have been? We filmed in New York. Two months of preproduction, with no rest on weekends. Four months of filming, Monday to Friday. All on location. We scouted the entire city. Manhattan, Brooklyn, Harlem, the Bronx, Queens. I asked the actors to live in the apartments where their characters lived. They complained, they thought it was crazy, but I convinced them. Sean Penn spent four months living in a studio in Harlem. Meryl Streep in her West Village mansion. Although a mansion in the West Village is just a big house anywhere else in the world—this one wasn't even a house, it was an apartment building converted into a house. I asked the location manager how much the place would cost and he told me it was seventeen million. I moved into a three-bedroom apartment with a view of Central Park. I don't know why the three bedrooms. Hilario never came to visit me. Before getting started on preproduction, I spent a few days in Punta del Este. They treated me great, so great they made me feel unnecessary. They said yes to everything, like you would to a crazy man. I think they'd planned it. Hilario played his role to perfection: son of the asshole. My ex asked me over breakfast how the movie was coming along. I could tell she wasn't interested. None of the three of them was the slightest bit interested in what I might be doing with my life. A ghost. A deplorable ghost. A white shit-stained sheet with two holes for eyes. One night, while they were asleep, I put the few things I'd brought with me into the carry-on and I went to stay at the Conrad. Continental breakfast, a swim, that same afternoon a drive to Montevideo, then a plane to New York. Filming was a joy. First time in my life I didn't go over budget. Not one setback with the actors. Of the eighty-eight days of filming, only once did we go overtime. I had lunch on Mondays with the actors, Tuesdays with the DP and his team, Wednesdays with the costume designer and her team, Thursdays with the makeup artist and her team, Fridays with the assistant director and the interns. On weekends I went out on the town with the Universal people, and the financiers if they came to visit. Sunday mornings I went for bike rides in Central Park, at noon I'd eat a burger at the Corner Bistro, I bought records on Bleecker Street. Four months of pure pleasure. The first time I've ever enjoyed filming, Pablo. I invited my mother to spend a few days in New York with me. She stayed at my apartment. She sat behind me at the video assist in the morning, because after lunch she started to fall asleep and I'd ask my driver to take her back to the apartment so she could take a nap.

The woman next to me just woke up and asked me where we were. Close, I told her.

I hired Pablo Barbieri, the best Argentine editor, for post-production, said Santiago. I thought about setting up an editing suite here in San Martín, in one of the empty bedrooms upstairs. But in the end we worked in Los Angeles. Constant twenty-five degrees Celsius. Barbieri and I laughed a lot. Although the need to have the movie ready before Cannes put a little pressure on us. We started to work at night, after dinner, from eleven to four in the morning. I talked to Thierry Frémaux and he told me not to worry, to forget about the deadline and send the finished movie straight to him. In spite of the script's hundred thirty-nine pages, the edited movie fit perfectly into a hundred and twenty minutes. Another miracle. First time I didn't go over two hours. One hundred nineteen minutes and thirty-three seconds, credits included. Written and directed by Santiago Salvatierra. Music by Philip Glass. Director of photography, Claudio Miranda. (Pause.) When Frémaux called to tell me that the movie had gotten into Un Certain Regard, I felt film history turning its back on me. A film history that had always talked to me face-to-face was now turning its back on me and talking to me without even turning its head. I thanked him, told him it was an honor, and started thinking about what excuse I could give to get out of that shitty festival.

The bus is stuck in traffic that I look down on from my window.

Streets that dream of San Martín de los Andes the way I used to dream about Santa Claus's snowy house when I was little.

Anita, hand in hand with a man who knocks down trees with his head.

I went to Greece, said Santiago. I wanted to get away from the movie. It was ready, edited, color corrected, the sound mix all wrapped up. Before I left, I invited the actors to the Universal screening room and showed them the final cut. They reacted coldly. Only Sean tried to convince me it was a masterpiece. Have fun in Greece, he told me, you deserve a vacation, forget yourself, forget everything, when you get back we'll dive into promotion. Meryl got a phone call and went out to the parking lot to talk and I never saw her come back. Jennifer told me she was going to have sushi for lunch with two friends and asked me if I wanted to come, but I said no, thanks, I have plans. I didn't have any plans. Jack spent the whole movie rolling with laughter, and there's not much to laugh at in that movie. At the end he told me: "Funny, funny stuff," and he left.

The bus isn't moving anymore; it inches along but doesn't move forward.

The pilot or driver is sharing a *mate* with the copilot or codriver.

I spent three months living at the Chateau Marmont, in one of the bungalows around the pool, said Santiago. I did nothing but sleep, swim, and eat. I never left the hotel. I didn't watch movies or TV. I tried to reread *Other Inquisitions*, but I couldn't get past "Pascal's Sphere." I read "The Wall and the Books" about seventy times. I put on workout clothes and walked to the gym and grabbed a towel and programmed the treadmill and right away I turned it off and threw the towel in the basket and went back to my bungalow. I jerked off ninety times. I dialed Hilario's number ninety times, and all ninety times I hung up before it rang. We started the promotion campaign at the end of August. Tons of posters plastered up everywhere. The trailer on YouTube, Facebook, on TV, taxi screens. I gave interviews to *Variety*, the *Hollywood Reporter*, *Deadline*, the

New York Times, the *L.A. Times*, the *Huffington Post*. I appeared on
Colbert. One week before the premiere, the actors went on all the
talk shows, morning and night. Jennifer hosted *Saturday Night Live*.
On Tuesday we held a press screening. They asked me to do a Q
and A, but I said no. I didn't even show my face in the theater. On
Friday morning the reviews appeared. No one called me. No one
tried to convince me that critics today don't influence audiences,
that they don't have any weight. No one invited me to a bar so we
could get good and drunk and . . . (Pause.) On Rotten Tomatoes:
seven fresh reviews, sixty-four rotten ones. Almost all the reviews,
good and bad, had glowing words for the script. Its originality. A
new force. That it doesn't completely work, but it opens doors. A
funereal silence waiting for nominations. The people at Universal
told me they were doing everything possible. They begged me to
go to dinners at the Academy, drinks with the Foreign Press Association. I went back to New York. I didn't leave the hotel. A chain
called Dream, Dream Hotels, which is like living in a South Beach
club. But I didn't ask them to move me to another one. I walked
around the Meatpacking District looking for stupid shit to buy. I
took three showers a day. I put on my bathing suit, sunglasses, and
robe, and went down to the pool, and if there was anyone there,
in the water or sunbathing, even if it was just one person, even if
they were asleep on a lounge chair, I went back to my room. Nominations were presented by actors on CBS at eight in the morning Eastern time. I didn't turn on the TV. I stayed in bed, under
the comforter, cracking my knuckles. No one called me. Neither
of the two mornings. Later I read in *Variety* that only Meryl had
been nominated, for Best Supporting Actress. I stayed in New York
another month, in an apartment in Hell's Kitchen with a view of
the Hudson. I spoke only Spanish. I bought sandwiches in a deli on
Forty-Third and Tenth, and I chatted for a while with the Mexican

cook, Antonio, a thirtysomething father whose wife and five kids lived in Matamoros; he was only a little taller than the counter. I had my left knee checked out; it cracks when I bend it. The Writers Guild of America paid. The doctor recommended I operate. I didn't understand exactly what the problem was. One night I had dinner with Manu Ginóbili at an Argentine restaurant in Alphabet City. He told me he had seen the movie and liked it. I didn't believe him. At the Strand I bought all seven volumes of Proust. I set out to read one a week, a hundred pages a day. I didn't get past page twelve of Volume I. In Europe we got better reviews. France thought the movie was interesting. Italy not so much. England ignored us, not a single BAFTA nomination. In Spain they nominated us for a Goya, I don't remember what category. They begged me to go to the ceremony, but I said . . . Health problems. Again with the pneumonia. I don't know. (Pause.) Tomorrow it premieres here in Argentina. No one knows I came to San Martín. My publicist told the press I was on vacation in Greece. Knossos.

There's no longer any rhythm or melody to the fingernail against the glass, a simple *ta ta ta ta ta ta ta ta* to drive me crazy.

I just saw a movie poster at a bus stop; I thought I saw Meryl Streep's face, although Streep tends to work on several films a year.

Before I came down to the basement, I talked to Hilario for a while, said Santiago. He told me he still hadn't seen the movie, that it comes out next week in Punta del Este. I think he was lying. Hilario downloads everything he watches and listens to from the Pirate Bay, and the movie's been on that site for a while now. Hundreds of thousands of downloads. Hundreds of thousands of people who don't pay what they should pay so art can go on being what it . . . Millions of people who stuck their hands into my pocket and robbed me, and who don't have the balls to show their faces and admit they're thieves. The internet is going to end up destroying everything. Not just art, everything. This false idea that the internet encourages democracy, that it gives power to the people. Okay, maybe in a way it's true, it does grant a certain amount of power to the people—but what people? Most people are anti-artistic. Most people are lazy as shit. Not just around here, no, all over the world. The internet gave power to the people, and the people don't know what to do with that power other than vent their misery, their hatred, their rage, their feeble minds, their rotten souls. The internet, with the help of Facebook and the others, told people: You all are artists, you are, and your lives are works of art, they're movies and books, they're your paintings, your sculptures, your plays, so forget about movies and books, forget about paintings, sculptures, and plays, and look at yourselves, show yourselves. And those pathetic people listened, they ate that shit up, and they spend their lives looking at themselves and showing themselves, feeding off their shitty art that isn't art, an art that is killing art, a nothing so fascinating that . . . And at the same time they fill the pockets of the sons of bitches who invented the game, who convinced them that . . . that they . . . that . . .

FINAL DRAFT FILE

A café across from the multiplex cinema on the corner of Vuelta de Obligado and Mendoza.

I found a table at the back next to the only wall with a three-prong plug.

The movie starts in an hour.

The theater's almost full, according to the ticket seller.

Though it's already night, I ordered a *café con leche* with three croissants—the only three left, one of them fairly burnt.

I don't know why, when the waiter brought me the menu (a menu that includes a suspiciously out-of-place mushroom risotto), the first thing I thought of was a *café con leche* with croissants.

I'm fifteen blocks away from my old lady's apartment.

The neighborhood hasn't changed much.

Seven years in a basement that belongs to a dream.

A dream that should be a nightmare.

A bittersweet dream.

Not one of those dreams you wake up from and desperately want to return to.

A dream that's better left behind, but not one I'm scared of, not one that's going to hound me for the rest of my life, lurking in mirrors and behind slightly open doors.

A dream that's maybe a gift from the no longer all-time greatest film director in Latin America or the world.

The croissants are only worthwhile if I dip them in the *café con leche*.

Three seconds of *café con leche* turns the glaze into a treat.

It drips from the corners of my mouth.

I used five paper napkins.

The ticket is also paper; they still use paper tickets.

Thousands of trees cut down so that thousands of bored people can enter thousands of movie theaters and see thousands of shitty movies.

I use the word "shit" a lot.

Did Santiago use the word "shit" a lot?

I use the phrase "a lot" a lot.

Santiago will soon be shit.

Did Norma call Santiago's ex-wife, his son, his mother?

Santiago's mother is one of those people who make your hair stand on end when you see them in a photo.

Many faces spill from the theater onto the sidewalk, but it's really only one: the face of a person who has visited a fortune-teller, but didn't hear the prophesy they were hoping for.

I could stand in the theater doorway, beside the man or woman who tears the tickets and hands out programs, to tell each of the viewers that I wrote the movie, this movie, the one they're about to see; that Santiago Salvatierra kidnapped me and kept me locked in a basement against my will and forced me to write screenplays for him, although not this screenplay, no no, the screenplay that was used to film this movie they're about to see is not the result of the kidnapping, no, no no no no, the screenplay used for the movie they're about to see arose from the . . . from the . . . from a . . . from an . . . no no no.

Theater 1, the largest.

A line of people that lengthens as my *café con leche* gets cold.

Is it disrespectful to buy popcorn when you're going to see a movie that was supposed to change the course of world cinema history and didn't?

Beckett changed the course of world literary history with works that weren't supposed to change anything; that is, they were conceived (conceived?) . . . *written* without any intention to change fuck-all.

They changed the history of world literature because they deserved to change it, not because they were *supposed* to change it.

Although now that I think about it, I'm not sure, maybe Beckett did write those works with the intention of changing the history of world literature, since those works (especially his trilogy that isn't a trilogy) strive to annihilate the novel, and the story, and even the philosophical essay, once and for all.

Beckett would never have agreed to cowrite screenplays with directors who didn't know how to write; he would never have agreed to cowrite at all, but that only comes from not understanding the nature of the film, which is the collaborative art par excellence.

I never expected Santiago to give me the credit "Written by" alone, I certainly never demanded it; I only hoped, wished (I certainly didn't demand) that he would put my name under his: "Written by Santiago Salvatierra and Pablo Betances," or "Santiago Salvatierra & Pablo Betances."

In this third screenplay they could have (should have) inverted the names: "Written by Pablo Betances & Santiago Salvatierra."

Pablo Salvatierra & Santiago Betances.

Pablo Santiago & Betances Salvatierra.

Betances Salvatierra sounds like a major-league baseball player.

The good thing about sports is that no athlete can claim a success he didn't achieve motu proprio.

Sanpablo Salvances & Tiago Betierra.

The problem is that Santiago needed the credit of "Written and directed by"; he needed it enough to kidnap a stranger and force him to write at gunpoint.

The movie's original title is *Ad fundum*, which in Latin means "toward the core" or "to the depths."

I guess Santiago must have fought to keep them from changing it when it was translated; he must have argued with the worldwide distributors the way he did with his previous movies, imploring them—no, *compelling* them—to leave the title alone.

But here in Argentina they were having none of that, and the movie at the Multiplex Belgrano is called *Abriéndose camino* (Making Way).

Santiago used Latin expressions for several of his movies; my favorite one, the title I like the most, is *Quidam*, which means "someone," but someone of little importance, an indeterminate someone.

A line of *quidams* waiting to see my movie.

I paid for the *café con leche* and croissants with Santiago's credit card.

I thought about running away when the waiter walked off with the card, but I stayed still, not typing anything, my eyes on the laptop reading what I'd written but not really reading, convinced that the police were about to barge into the café with machine guns and bulletproof vests.

I hear church bells in the distance.

No, it's the cell phone of the waiter who is coming back with Santiago's card and my receipt.

A man at the next table over ordered the mushroom risotto; it looks good.

Santiago left the waiter a forty percent tip, then took out the revolver and aimed it at me.

Is it "mushroom risotto" or "risotto with mushrooms"?

If *risotto* just means "rice," then it should be "risotto with mushrooms."

If *risotto* refers to the whole dish, then it would be "mushroom risotto."

I could ask the waiter.

I don't know why I put my hands up, as if I were in a bank and a totally bald thief had come in to rob it.

Put your hands down, said Santiago.

Lower the gun and I will, I told him.

What did you do?

When?

What did you change in the way you . . . ? What was it that convinced me? The most incredible thing is that I didn't even doubt for a second. I went to sleep that night convinced, and the next day I read it again and I was convinced again. No, I wasn't convinced again, because I was already convinced; I read it again and my conviction got stronger. But that script was a trick. You tricked me, Pablo. I don't know how, and that's what I need you to explain to me. Is that what you were doing all these years? Learning how to trick me? Studying me? Reading me? Was it always so hot in this basement?

I tried to explain to him that . . . to start explaining that . . . although I didn't know exactly what it was I had to explain . . . but Santiago interrupted me and told me that clearly my greatest talent was deception.

You're not an artist, Pablo, he said. You're an illusionist. That script was a card trick. I never would have imagined when I hired you that—

You *hired* me? Where is that contract, Santiago? What's my salary? I never got the checks.

He brought the revolver closer to my face.

This is the contract. Here inside is your signature, your name. I only have to spin it to find out what your salary is.

He spun the chamber.

Again.

Again.

Again.

You know what most fucked me up? he asked. How the financiers, who for the first time ever didn't pay a single extra peso, got so frugal after they saw the film, so full of clichés, so . . . No, that's not what fucked me up the most. What most fucked me up was not realizing. Not having realized.

While Santiago spoke, his gun hand was rotating at the wrist, the barrel pointing toward random corners of the basement.

If the critics say that the only salvageable thing about a movie is the script, he said, then the only worthless thing is the script. Whatever the critics praise is the worst part, always the worst, and whatever they criticize is the best part, always the best. Critics function in reverse. We should watch the movies that rotted on Rotten Tomatoes. Only rotten movies, the ones that reek of burst abscesses.

It starts in twenty minutes; I'm going to miss the trailers.

Why are trailers called trailers in English?

Trailers are mobile homes.

I could go online and see the trailer for *Ad fundum*.

I can't go online, the laptop's Wi-Fi doesn't work.

If I could connect, I'd have checked my email, googled what they said in the press after I disappeared, how long the search lasted; I could have googled my old lady, though most likely I wouldn't have found anything, because my mother, like me, doesn't exist on the internet; that is, she doesn't exist.

Enough.

I'm going to leave the café and make my way.

To the depths.

MOVIE PROGRAM

I found a pen on the floor.
I'm writing in the right margin
of an ad for the new Woody Allen movie,
written and directed by Woody Allen,
starring Woody Allen.
Who needs another Woody Allen movie?
Who needs another movie?
I didn't buy popcorn.
A couple sitting to my right
are devouring handfuls of popcorn
from a plastic bucket
with *Toy Story* characters.
Popcorn is *pochoclo* in Argentina.
Pochoclo always reminds me of
Achilles's gigolo friend in the *Iliad*.
I use the word "always" a lot.
How easily we say "always" and "never."
I've already written this elsewhere.
The last trailer is over
and the cartoon cell phone

225

pleads with us to put
our devices on silent.
I don't have a cell phone.
There should be a cartoon popcorn bucket or a jaw
that pleads with people eating popcorn
to put their jaws on silent.
The lights go out.
They'd already been dimmed
after the commercials
and before the trailers.
The theater's dark, but not completely.
I see the curtains on either side
as they open farther
and expand the screen.
A film not fit for minors under 13.
PG-13.
The Universal logo.
Black.
Sounds of traffic.
Ad fundum.
Below, subtitled:
Abriéndose camino.
Wide shot on a New York avenue.
Another movie that starts with
a wide shot on a New York avenue.
Half of all Hollywood movies
start with a wide shot
of a New York avenue.
How did the screenplay open?
What was the first shot,
or the first heading?

THE CROSSED-OUT NOTEBOOK

Luckily the words "New York"
don't appear on the screen.
I hate it when they show
the name of the city on the screen,
or the year
the scene occurs in.
Enough with treating the viewer
like a stupid baby.
In the next two hours
the history of world cinema
is not going to change.

YELLOW STICKY NOTE

Two in the morning.

I'm sitting in the doorway of the building typing this on a yellow sticky on the laptop.

The sticky note can be blue, green, pink, gray, or yellow.

They're called "stickies" in Spanish: "las stickies."

I don't know why I say "*las* stickies" and not "*los* stickies"; are sticky notes female?

I came out of the theater at eleven forty-five and walked slowly to the apartment building.

It was hard to get up the nerve to buzz the apartment.

I thought about stopping a woman who was coming out and asking her about my old lady, but I let her go by and head to the corner, where she hailed a taxi.

The electric intercom is different.

I think it's different.

My hand was shaking when I touched the 4B button.

No one answered.

I waited.

I buzzed again.

No one.

I waited.

I buzzed again.

No one.

No one went in or out.

I thought about buzzing a different apartment, but for some reason I didn't.

The temperature went way down: the ground is freezing, like the glass of the door I'm leaning against.

The laptop's back on my lap like in the old days of the basement.

Not too many people walking past on the sidewalk.

The few people who do pass want to attack me and steal the laptop, but at the last moment they think better of it and go on walking as if they hadn't seen me.

No one sees me.

It's likely that when my old lady arrives she'll go right past me and into the apartment without noticing I'm here, on the ground, typing about her, about fear, so much fear, Ma.

Nineteen percent battery.

The day my mother was born: November 19.

My father was born on April 13, the same day Samuel Beckett was born, only forty years later.

Maybe one of the people who walked by was Lisandro.

Does he still live around the corner?

I could go and ring his doorbell.

I could go and ring all the doorbells on the block, wake up the neighborhood, scream the truth at them, tell them Santiago fucked me over, fucked us all, fucked himself.

Ad fundum was not directed by Santiago Salvatierra.

I don't know who got behind that camera.

An impostor.

*   *   *

How could I convince myself that a script completely rewritten in a few days was ready to be filmed? asked Santiago.

Hours, I said.

What?

I already told you, I wrote it in an afternoon/evening and early morning. Twelve hours. One hundred and thirty-nine pages in twelve hours.

He aimed the gun between my legs.

You say it like you were proud.

No. Because I don't know what I wrote in those twelve hours. You can't be proud of something unknown. I *am* proud of having escaped my lethargy and paralysis, of having sat down to write and not stopped until I finished. But what it is you read that Monday morning, I don't have the slightest idea. The truth is—stop aiming at my balls—the truth is, I thought you'd gone to work with another screenwriter, that you'd abandoned me, and that Norma was going to come down any minute and kill me with a bullet to the head.

He spun the chamber and aimed at the rectangle of light and pulled the trigger.

Click.

There's no other screenwriter, he said. I'm the only screenwriter. You type and I write. That movie was already written, Pablo. I served it up to you on a platter. You only had to type it, the same way you typed the two scripts before. I gave you time. Two weeks. Two weeks to type the third act and half of the—

Enough, Santiago. You can think whatever you want, imagine whatever you want, you didn't write those scripts. *I* wrote them. I did. Not you, not Peter Shaffer, not Aristotle. Me. The fucker whose balls you're aiming at. The scripts are both of ours, yours and mine, but I wrote them. I chose every word. I chose every scene heading and action and parenthetical and line of dialogue. Arguing over a scene for two hours is not writing it. It's being part of the scene. That is, the scene may belong partly to you. But that's not the same as writing it. You don't understand what it is to sit for hours in front of a blank page, like a stupid kid looking at a Miró painting of nothing, waiting for—

I don't know? You think I never tried? Day after day after day. But that's not what's important. You're confused, Pablo. Writing the script isn't writing it. The script is nothing but a guide for a movie. A movie I had in my head long before you wrote it. A movie that I gave you so you could write it. You put the words of the movies in my head so that I could film them, so the members of my crew would understand the movies in my head, the movies that all of us together had to get onto sixteen- or thirty-five-millimeter film or onto a camera's hard drive. What people see in the movie theater is a shadow of a shadow. And the saddest thing of all, what breaks my heart every time I finish filming a movie, is to know that people will never even glimpse the original movie, the one that was in my head, a film that is infinitely superior to that third version they see in the theater. Haneke said that if he finished a movie and it was forty percent of what he had in his head he was the happiest man in the world. He didn't say "happy." Haneke would never use the word "happy." I don't know what word he'd use.

He smiled, and pointed the gun at my face.

You know why I kill myself working on each of my movies?

I kept quiet; it wasn't a question Santiago intended for me to answer.

Because I know that if I don't kill myself working then the movie will be a farce, he said, a cheap imitation of something glorious. I kill myself working because it's the only way to get sixty percent of the original out into the world. Give people sixty percent. Less than sixty percent is a farce. Haneke's films are farces. Exceptional farces, incredibly well-made, fabulously written, directed, and acted farces. Never less than sixty percent, Pablo.

Never until now.

The movie I have just seen, *Ad fundum*, *Abriéndose camino*, *Making Way*, is not even thirty percent of my screenplay.

Santiago didn't kill himself working on the movie that was supposed to change the course of world cinema history.

It's not possible that he killed himself working on the movie I have just seen.

It's one of those perfectly made movies, perfectly directed and acted, perfectly edited, perfectly lit, that at the same time aren't worth anything; in other words, the worst kind of movie.

It's better to make a piece of shit, a movie that makes people furious, than to make something mediocre.

I don't know if "mediocre" is the right word.

It's a good movie, very good in some respects, and at the same time it's insignificant.

A movie that has everything it needs to work, but doesn't work.

The only thing not perfectly made is the screenplay.

The screenplay fails left and right, but at the same time it's the only thing with any life in that movie.

The filming of that screenplay was an embalming.

A living and imperfect body was converted into a dead and perfect body; it's eternal—eternally useless.

Humankind's obsession with making eternal works of art, when someday they're going to go extinct like the dinosaurs.

Except for Lennon's "Tomorrow Never Knows."

We're all going to go extinct.

My old lady, Lisandro, Norma, and Paul McCartney.

Yoko Ono in a shrill howl of stupidity.

My screenplay deserved to be directed by the best Santiago Salvatierra.

No, the best Fellini, probably the greatest director of all time; an immense and incomparable artist who, like Santiago, understood his job as director to be like Christopher Columbus's job commanding a crew who only wants to turn around.

Fellini knew how to collaborate with more than one screenwriter.

La dolce vita was cowritten by five people, including the ghost collaboration of Pasolini.

8½ was cowritten by four people.

Amarcord by two.

Ginger and Fred by three.

And no one has devalued Fellini as an artist for having shared the credit of "Written by" with one, two, three, or even four people.

* * *

Fifteen percent battery.

Someone across the street is listening to Vilma Palma e Vampiros.

Santiago asked me if the ukelele with only three strings didn't run the risk of getting out of tune.

The revolver in his right hand had seemingly ceased to exist.

He took several steps back, peered around the basement again, then looked straight at me with eyes that were suddenly full of tears.

He wanted to say something to me.

Maybe to apologize.

Accept that he had committed a crime, an atrocity, an act that belonged in a Haneke movie, one from his Austrian period, and not in reality.

But that wasn't reality.

At least, not the reality of this cold ground.

Santiago had invented his own reality, a world that danced around him, bowed to his rules.

What did we do, Pablo? he asked me. Ninety-seven million, over fifty on publicity. We made a fucking mess. Me leaving you alone so many days, you scratching your balls until the last night . . . okay, afternoon and night . . . and early morning . . . me accepting as final a draft that was far from final. But everyone loved the script. And that confused me even more. You fooled us all. You fooled a large portion of Hollywood. You fooled the Turkish financiers, guys who earn fortunes selling arms and other things it's better not to even know about. Did you do it on purpose? Was it your way of getting revenge? Why the hell did you write that script?

He pressed the gun to my head.

Pulled the trigger.

Click.

My legs were shaking.

I did what I could to keep my teeth from chattering.

I thought about grabbing his wrist, kicking him in the balls, kneeing him in the liver.

If you did it on purpose I understand, Pablo, he said. I'll never, ever forgive you for it, but I'll understand.

He spun the chamber, aimed between my eyes, pulled the trigger.

Click.

I didn't do anything on purpose, I said. I just wrote the best script I could in one afternoon/evening and early morning. I had to put aside everything we'd done in order to write it. The structuring of the story was a dike five kilometers thick that wouldn't let the words flow. I had to get naked. I had to hammer at the dike and break it and I had to get naked and . . .

Click.

Ad fundum is a movie you forget quickly.

I'm sure that Santiago wanted it that way.

He wanted it without realizing.

Unconsciously, he threw the movie off a cliff.

He strove to achieve the highest degree of insignificance possible, the purest insignificance, because from the start he knew it didn't belong to him.

Neither of the previous screenplays had belonged to him, either, but this time he knew it.

He admired what he read, and he tried to convince himself that it belonged to him, that it had come from inside him, but he couldn't convince himself.

When he called "Action," he knew that the scene he was about to direct was my scene, and then he stood behind it and pushed it gently off a cliff.

A scene in a wheelchair falling into . . .

Click.

He started to hit himself on his right temple with the butt of the gun.

Hilario must have seen it by now, he said. And he doesn't answer my calls, or reply to my emails. My son is no longer my son, Pablo. He decided to stop being my son.

He spun the chamber, pointed at my chest, and pulled the trigger.

Click.

No cars are passing.

A black cat jumped from the only tree in sight and dubiously crept closer to me, and stopped, and abruptly turned and fused with the night's blackness.

In Buenos Aires, the black of night is not black.

The basement could be completely black and silent, so black

and silent that the walls and ceiling stopped existing; I could walk in a straight line for hours without hitting anything.

The lights had gone out in Santiago's head.

I don't know how long he spent repeating himself, spinning the chamber and pulling the trigger, *click*; blaming me for having tricked him, blaming everyone who had worked on the movie that was supposed to change the course of world cinema history and did not change it.

Hours and hours of preproduction, he said, and no one came to tell me I was making a mistake.

While he was aiming at me and spouting words, I was imagining a tiny version of Santiago pacing around the dark room that was his mind—the same mind that was holding the gun—and I imagined that tiny Santiago taking little steps in a circle, humming a lullaby he used to sing to his son, Hilario, when he had trouble falling asleep.

I wonder if Spinetta sang lullabies to his kids—the most beautiful lullabies in the world, his icicle voice dripping as it melted above a warmly lit home.

The people in the theater practically made no sound during the movie's two hours.

No laughter or sobs or sighs.

Just jaws chewing popcorn.

A cough.

Three people left before the end of the second act.

Meryl Streep is the only one of the actors who took ownership of her character and gave her some life.

I would have liked to meet the woman Meryl Streep plays in the movie.

There are several characters in the history of world cinema I would have liked to meet, more than I would have liked to meet the actors who played those characters.

Antonio Salieri.

Barton Fink.

Guido Anselmi.

Annie Hall.

Tom Hagen.

Erika Kohut.

Frank the Tank.

Dorothy Vallens.

*   *   *

Maybe they'll honor me at Argentores.

Maybe Argentores will get me a lawyer and I can sue Santiago's heirs—though I'm not sure Argentores hires lawyers for penniless writers who need them.

Santiago owes me a fortune.

It would have been so easy for him to send part of the screenwriter's fees I should have earned to my mother.

I understand it's a problem to justify having an anonymous person give thousands of dollars to a middle-class woman in Buenos Aires, but in any case it could have been my mother's decision what to do with the money: keep it and not make a peep, give it away, or report it to the police.

Although if my mother had received a bag with thousands of dollars from a stranger, most likely she would have thought it had something to do with me, that I was the one who'd sent the money, and she wouldn't have been able to live in peace, rebuilding her life without me.

I hope with all my soul that my old lady rebuilt her life after I disappeared.

And now I'll be forcing her to re-rebuild it.

Or no, to go back to before, to what we were before Santiago, but better, because the tragedy is going to unite us even more, it's going to allow us to enjoy our life without luxury and feel at the same time like the richest people in the world.

No, it's ridiculous to go back to what we were before.

Santiago had to die so that I . . .

Santiago could no longer look at his face in the mirror; it was a face that didn't want to punch his lights out, no, and that didn't invite him to punch its lights out, no; it was a face that simply laughed and laughed at him.

There'd be nothing left for him after killing me.

Santiago betrayed everything he was because he couldn't accept . . .

Salieri betrayed everything he was because he couldn't accept that he was not the composer who composed melodies for God.

But after he drove a sick Mozart to his death by forcing him to work on the *Requiem*, his own *Requiem*, Mozart's (though Mozart didn't know it was his own *Requiem*, no, for him it was a simple commission; or no, not so simple, because he needed the money, and the commission came from an unknown figure who had appeared to him in the mask of his dead father), he had no other option than to go crazy (Salieri), or pretend to be crazy and flee his place in the world, a place of privilege.

Would I have preferred for Santiago to kill me?

No.

No?

No.

Now it's my time to live.

Not *live like before*, I can't live like that anymore.

My smells are not the same anymore.

If my mother still exists, it's likely she wouldn't recognize me with her eyes closed.

My hemorrhoids are throbbing.

I forgot the chewable pills.

Nine percent battery.

Nine is three threes.

I'd like to go for a bike ride—on a mountain bike, because the other kind breaks your ass, and my ass is already broken by hemorrhoids.

Does my old lady have hemorrhoids?

Everyone has hemorrhoids.

A couple of bright red hemorrhoids hang off planet Earth: the Falklands.

I get up and buzz the intercom again.

If no one answers, I'll wake a neighbor.

I hope Norma left Santiago's body on the basement floor and split for Mexico.

More likely she's still on her knees scrubbing blood from the floor and the walls and the rectangle of light, the poor rectangle that kept me company all that time.

I should build one in the bedroom.

Tomorrow I'm going to go to an internet café to print the screenplay about the boy who throws his family into a well, and then I'm going to call Lisandro and tell him what happened, and after a lot of hugs and crying I'm going to ask him to give me the phone numbers and addresses of the best film producers in Buenos Aires.

There's no need to go to an internet café and print the screenplay about the boy who throws his family into a well; I can ask Lisandro for the email addresses of the best film producers in Buenos Aires and send them a PDF copy with a dedication on the first page:

"To Santiago Salvatierra, the greatest Latin American film director of all time."

*   *   *

Eight percent.

I've just realized, as I'm typing this, that I can't stop typing.

It fills me with panic to be free of the obligation to write in this crossed-out notebook that hasn't been a crossed-out notebook for some time now.

This is what I am, really: these few rushed pages.

I no longer know what I am outside these pages.

I'm too terrified to find out.

Even the screenplay of *Ad fundum* was written in these pages that are no longer pages.

This *text*.

I should copy the entire screenplay and paste it in the middle of this miserable text, a text that is cowardly but real, more real than the reality outside it.

Crossed-Out Notebook is a good title.

How do you say *The Crossed-Out Notebook* in Latin?

Beckett lives in the paragraphs of his trilogy that isn't a trilogy, and his life outside those paragraphs doesn't matter.

Jack Nicholson's life offscreen doesn't matter.

Meryl Streep's life offscreen doesn't matter.

Great actors know how to get into the scenes and live, to be themselves in those preexisting scenes.

That's what I have to do now: be myself in a preexisting reality, get into a scene that was filmed some time ago and try to find my place, find it again; or get into myself, the version of me that I was before the basement, and try to find my place, find it again.

Santiago asked me again why I had written the screenplay.

I didn't know how to answer beyond:

Because it's all I know how to do.

He spun the chamber, aimed at my face, and pulled the trigger. *Click.*

He spun the chamber, aimed at my face, and pulled the trigger. *Click.*

He spun the chamber, aimed at my face, and pulled the trigger. *Click.*

He spun the chamber, aimed at my face, and pulled the trigger. *Click.*

I burst into tears.

Santiago stood still, watching me spill tears and snot.

Silence.

I thought I could hear Norma on the other side of the door: she said something that neither of us understood, not that I have any way of knowing if Santiago understood it or not.

I supposed that maybe the best thing to do was to tell Santiago that yes, he was right, I had written a screenplay that was a trick, a card trick, to screw him over, to take revenge, but I didn't say that because it wasn't true, I had written the best screenplay possible, the best scenes possible in those few hours of afternoon, night, and early morning, to help him, with the intention that together we could change the course of world cinema history, even if no one would ever know we had done it together; I put the best of me in those pages, sitting on that floating mattress, because I wasn't in the basement while I wrote those pages, those scenes, I wasn't anywhere other than in those pages, those scenes, those characters, those dialogues that flowed out of me like an interminable piss, the most pleasurable piss, the kind of piss you hold until you almost explode, and that when you let it out, you free yourself of all the evils of the world.

I didn't tell him any of that.

My sobbing forced me to cough and it stopped up my ears, and Santiago's face, there, still, as he held the revolver, shook me even more, until I saw him spin the chamber again, and aim the gun at my face that was destroyed by tears, and my legs started to shake as they did every time Santiago pointed the gun at me, but he didn't fire, he aimed the gun at his own right temple, and he pulled the trigger, *click*, and he spun the chamber again, and aimed at me, and pulled the trigger, *click*, and he spun the chamber, aimed at himself, and pulled the trigger, *click*, and he spun the chamber, and aimed at me, and pulled the trigger, *click*, and he spun the chamber, aimed at himself, and pulled the trigger, *click*, and he spun the chamber, aimed at me, and pulled the trigger, *click*, and he spun the chamber, aimed at himself, and fired.

*　　*　　*

My sob cut off abruptly, as if some invisible person had slapped me.

I didn't want to look at Santiago's body.

It was impossible not to look at it.

I checked to see if he was dead: there was no pulse in his wrist or his neck.

The shot echoed, like it was waiting for the door to open and let it out.

But the door was locked.

Wasn't it?

I had never seen Santiago lock the door with a key.

Or Norma, either.

I assumed the door locked on its own: an automatic latch, a complex system, or not so complex but complex to me, like a high-security prison.

I walked to the closed door and turned the knob.

It opened easily.

It was always unlocked, I told myself. Always. For years, I'd refused to believe the door was unlocked. I'd convinced myself that the basement was a perfect cell.

No, I told myself, the door had always been locked. Always. Santiago left it unlocked yesterday morning, because somehow he knew the revolver was going to choose him. When he came down to the basement yesterday, he knew he wasn't going to come out alive.

He built the basement so he could lock me in and force me at gunpoint to write screenplays, plus six commercials (one for Apple, one for Samsung, one for Pepsi, three for Nike), without knowing that he was really building his own tomb.

No sign of Norma on the stairs.

When I put my foot onto the first step, I was afraid there'd be nothing at the top—an unfounded fear, perhaps, but one that paralyzed me, and the image of a staircase that went up and up and never got anywhere pushed me back down into the basement.

But the basement belonged to Santiago, to his lifeless body; it was the world's only burial chamber with a bathroom.

I had to look at him one last time, say goodbye, repress the urge to run over and give him a kick in the ass, a hundred kicks in the ass, so many I'd be sure that nothing of Santiago was left in that idiot body.

The universe at the top of the stairs still existed.

Here it is, surrounding me . . .

No, *holding me up*, the same way it holds up everything that lives and everything that doesn't.

A universe that, according to Santiago, hasn't changed artistically for a long time now.

I don't know if I'll be able to go back to my life from before.

Nor do I know if I'll be able to start a new life.

I don't know how I'm going to deal with my mother's nonexistence, if my mother no longer exists.

I don't know if I'm going to miss the basement, or if one day I'll look at myself in the mirror and discover that the basement is inside of me, that I am the basement.

All I know is that I'm capable of writing a good screenplay.

I don't know about a great one, but a good one, yes, much better than other screenplays that are considered good.

*   *   *

Five percent.

I don't know what I'm going to do when the battery runs out.

Find a bar with a table next to a three-prong plug?

No, I have to wait for my mother.

I'll take out the pen and keep writing, on my left arm.

I'm no longer capable of writing, at least not until I know what happened to my mother.

I can't yet be, exist, outside this formless, impossible text.

A text that could never be adapted into a screenplay.

I hope my old lady believes me when I tell her I wrote those screenplays.

I hope she believes me when I tell her I'm okay, that life in the basement wasn't hell, that the only things I lost were time and hair and those stones in my gallbladder that someone I don't know and will never meet took out while I was unconscious.

I have the unshakable feeling that if my old lady shows up and finds me sitting here, typing like a crazed monkey, she's going to ask me to get up, and she'll hug me as hard as she can, and that hug is going to be like the door to the basement, a basement that is me and that she's going to enter and never leave again.

Maybe I should stand up and walk away.

Just walk away.

*　　*　　*

Four percent.

In Santiago's bathroom I cleaned the spots of blood and brain from my neck and forehead, I scrubbed until they disappeared.

A crimson stitch on my earlobe.

I drank liters of water from the faucet.

I don't know if it was liters, but definitely several handfuls.

I don't know if "handfuls" is the right word.

What do you call the portion of water that you collect in your palms?

I thought about taking a shower, but it seemed disrespectful to shower with Norma crying in the kitchen.

I had developed a kind of sympathy for Norma, more so in the minutes since Santiago's suicide.

Suicide?

Is dying from Russian roulette suicide?

Santiago was murdered by his own revolver.

A revolver that he held in his own hand, that he himself pointed at his own right temple, with a chamber that he spun himself, but that . . . that is, it was the revolver that decided to kill him, that decided that Santiago, and not I, had to die.

I should have proposed marriage to Norma, brought her with me to the Capital; I'd sleep in the king-sized bed with Norma and my old lady, one on either side of me.

In the morning, my mother would prepare my instant coffee with milk, and Norma my little dish of fruit.

I should have stolen books from Santiago's library.

Beckett's trilogy that isn't a trilogy, although I doubt Santiago had it.

I could have started to read it now, when the battery runs out.

Three percent.

The light from the ground floor is more than enough to read by.

I'm going to put in the Califone earphones and listen to the Beatles discography, in order, until someone runs me over.

There are no cars, no pedestrians.

There are no lights in the slice of building I can see across the street.

Harrison sings "Do You Want to Know a Secret."

Like an idiot, it didn't occur to me that the music was going to eat up what's left of the battery.

One percent.

Three songs, Santiago would have insisted.

Someone is looking at me.

I think it's the doorman.

I don't say anything to him because I'm typing this on the yellow sticky note.

"A Taste of Honey."

A piece of toast with butter and honey; bite into a corner and mix it in my mouth with instant coffee with milk.

The *chile poblano* is in the past.

No, in my hemorrhoids.

The doorman—I don't know if he's a doorman—is talking to me.

I don't look up because I have to type this that I'm typing right now.

I type that I have to type this that I'm typing right now.

"There's a Place."

Lennon's voice is a furiously white basement in which to live.

The doorman is going to put a hand on my shoulder.

I hit the keys with letters that write on the yellow sticky that the doorman's hand has just landed on my shoulder.

I guess the text will save on its own, there's no need to go to File and